S0-EKO-072

Horses Get Lonely Too

Horses Get Lonely Too

Jenny Hughes

Typeset by Roberta L Melzl
Editor: Bobbie Chase
Printed in Germany, 2010

ISBN: 978-1-934983-46-1
Stabenfeldt, Inc.
225 Park Avenue South
New York, NY 10003
www.pony4kids.com

Available exclusively through PONY.

Chapter One

"Sian!" My mom's voice was agitated. "Can you help?"

I stopped running the body brush over Marnie's sleek dappled shoulder, gave her a quick kiss on the nose, and stepped out of her stable.

"Where are you?" I looked around the neat, deserted yard.

"In Major's box," she now sounded strangely muffled, "and I'm stuck."

I ran quickly to the empty stable used for Major, an old ex-polo pony, when he came in from the field.

"I still can't see you –" I began as I craned my neck over the door.

"I'm here!" Mom was getting madder every minute and I could see why.

She was standing flattened against the wall with her left arm jammed awkwardly inside the stable's old-fashioned hayrack.

"Giselle was in here," she panted, her voice becoming muffled again as she crossed her right arm over her face in the struggle to free the other one. "She seemed to be trapped so I tried to help her out."

"She's not there now." Trying not to laugh, I pushed open the door and went in.

"Well I know that!" Mom said crossly. "As soon as I got my hand in here she fluttered across to the door and down into the yard."

Giselle is a chicken, one of fourteen we rescued from a factory farm.

"Keep still," I ordered, my lips still twitching. "And I'll ease your hand back through the slats."

It was tricky, trying to slide her fingers out of the narrow gap, but once I managed it she was able to release her whole arm.

"Oh thanks, Sian." She wriggled her fingers gratefully. "I was starting to think I was stuck there forever."

"You shouldn't have bothered in the first place." I grinned at her. "Giselle is smarter than she looks. She'd have gotten out on her own anyway."

"You never know," Mom said darkly. "Those poor chickens didn't lead a natural life before coming here so I'm never sure if they're going to work things out."

"Do you want me to check on them all before I go out for my ride?" I asked. "Or would you rather I stayed here in case one of them traps you again?"

"Cheeky." She swung her left arm experimentally. "No thanks, take off. That pony of yours needs the exercise."

As I grabbed Marnie's saddle and bridle from the tack room I saw Mom carefully counting the chickens that were happily pecking around in the vegetable garden at the back of our house.

"Are they all there?" I called and she waved and nodded.

"Sorry I had to leave you, Marnie my pet," I crooned as I went back into my pony's stable. "It was a chicken emergency."

Marnie put her soft nose against my face and blew gently into my hair.

"Yes, you're right." I often hold complete conversations with her. "Technically it was a 'my mother' crisis, but she's OK now and so is Giselle."

I slid the saddle cloth gently onto her back, making sure her fine, dappled hair lay flat, then placed the saddle carefully on it. Marnie is five years old and, unlike the rest of the animals here at Greylodge, she has known only kindness and proper training. As a result she is the sweetest, most wonderful pony in the world with absolutely no vices whatsoever (if you discount a tendency to buck VERY high out of sheer exuberance, but even that's only occasional). She stood beautifully as I prepared to mount, only giving a whicker of excitement when we headed for the big gate leading to the outside world. The last few days had been wet and wild, confining us to the riding ring behind the yard, so Marnie was looking forward to a trip out as much as I was. As she waited politely for me to lean down and open the gate, one of her companions in the big summer field called to her and she answered immediately.

"Good girl." I asked her to turn so I could shut the

gate behind us. "Just say goodbye and tell them all you'll see them later."

There are five rescued horses at Greylodge, all from homes that were cruel, uncaring or just inadequate in some way. Major, the ex-polo pony, is old and has a touch of arthritis, but he's very happy to wander through our lovely pastures with his friends, Gail, Fanfare and Danny who, though happy, are also quite elderly. Only Texas, a fine Quarter horse that Mom found starving in a cowshed, can be ridden, since he was nursed back to health by Mom and me. Texas only likes to go out only occasionally, and since Mom doesn't get much time, with her job plus caring for the horses, five dogs, three cats, two pigs, eight ducks and the aforementioned chickens, Marnie and I mostly go out alone. It's fine; my pony is great company and the countryside surrounding Greylodge is wonderful riding territory. Up in the woods behind the house I've made a jumping course, using natural things like ditches, streams and fallen trees, plus some fairly challenging fences constructed from piled up broken branches. Marnie even helps me build these, following me around patiently (I don't need to lead her – she just stays with me) as I cart armfuls of stuff from one spot to another. Our most ambitious jump consists of a big fallen oak with two smaller ones crossed against it, and my clever pony actually made that one possible by letting me tie the smaller trees to her saddle so she could drag them into position.

Today, though, we weren't heading for our "cross-country course," deciding instead to take a pipe-opening gallop to the top of a long, steep-ish hill. We warmed up properly of course, walking briskly, then trotting and finally cantering the stretch of turf leading to the hill. Marnie has beautiful manners, rarely pulling and never snatching at the bit, but I can always tell when she's raring to gallop. She just fizzes with suppressed energy like a firework about to explode. When I give her the gallop aids she lengthens her body and neck to flow into the glorious four-time beat, each leg lengthening too as she powers us both across the springy turf. It's the nearest thing to flying I've ever known, and I tuck my upper body behind her neck, streamlining our outline so that the two of us are almost one. I shout out loud with the sheer joy and exhilaration of the moment and know I'm the happiest person in the whole wide world. The slope is a long one, but Marnie loves to gallop its full length, her pace not wavering until I give her the half-halt signals as we approach the summit. She probably feels, as I do, that she could fly like this forever, but she responds immediately and by the time we reach the broad, flat expanse at the top she's cantering smoothly. Once we were walking I guided her toward my favorite viewpoint, a rocky outcrop overlooking the lovely valley below. It's a breathtaking sight of lush green fields and woods, laced through with the broad, sparkling ribbon of the river I can hear from my window at night. I guess I'm a bit biased since I live here, but Greylodge really is a beautiful place, and seeing it from up here always makes me tingle with pride.

"There's home." I pointed and Marnie whickered softly.

"Yes, I know." I patted her neck lovingly. "It's a pretty nice spot to live in. Aren't we lucky?"

She moved her head, her dark, intelligent eyes seeming to take in the glorious detail below.

"Now you're looking at Danelea." I leaned forward in the saddle and pointed again. "See that hedge there? That's the boundary between our land and Danelea's. Mom said she heard the house has just been bought by someone, so it'll be nice to have neighbors again."

Marnie blew down her nose and seemed to nod thoughtfully.

"Maybe the new people will have horses," I agreed. "Their fields aren't as big as ours, but there's still plenty of room."

My pony lifted her off-fore hoof and pawed the air a few times.

"OK," I said, convinced I understood her every gesture. "On the way back we'll go past the Danelea pastures and take a look."

I kept on chatting to her for the rest of the ride which, after several more canters and a couple of small jumps, included a cooling paddle in a stream gurgling its way to the river. Leaving the water, we turned left and followed a narrow trail that skirted the boundary walls of Danelea. The wall was quite high and very solid and I realized there wasn't really a spot where I could actually see into the neighboring property. I'd never tried to do this before. The house used to be owned by an elderly couple who didn't have children or horses or anything much at all to interest me. Now though, I wanted to be nosey, to get a good look inside the grounds and see if there was any sign of the new owners.

"A family would be best," I told my pony. "Say two boys and a girl, all crazy about horses, obviously."

Marnie's pretty gray ears flickered.

"We could ride out together, have races and play pony club games." I could see it all in my imagination. "And we'll have competitions, like jumping the cross-country course. Maybe their dad will even help build some real proper fences."

Marnie snorted as we passed Danelea's gates, which were firmly closed.

"Mm." I came reluctantly out of my daydream. "You're probably right. I bet another old couple bought the place, and they won't have any kids or pets and they'll complain about everything."

That last bit was unfair really. Mr. and Mrs. Golding, who used to live there, only ever complained once and that was when the pigs, Sweet pea and Honey, broke through the fence and trampled their immaculate lawn. Mom had soon placated the Goldings; getting the pigs out at once, fixing the fence so it never happened again and spending ages smoothing the lawn back to its former perfection. As long as the new people were nice and reasonable I didn't mind *who* they were, I told Marnie, and she swished her tail to show she agreed. At least I thought that was what she meant but in fact she was warning me that a car, a big, powerful car, was approaching. We were, of course, correctly positioned on the right side of the lane leading toward home and expected the car to pass us carefully as all local drivers do. This one didn't pass, but instead slowed down and drew alongside.

Its window slid down and a deep, slightly impatient voice said, "Hello. Are you from Greylodge?"

"Hello," I replied cheerily. "Yes, I'm on my way back there."

"Then I take it your parents are at home?"

"My mom is." I wasn't going to call down from my saddle that I didn't have a dad.

"Good." He pressed the button to close the car window again. "Then I'll probably see you in a few minutes."

I stared at the expensive looking car as it moved smoothly away, and patted Marnie's neck thoughtfully. She, of course, was still walking out beautifully at the going-home, cooling-down pace I'd asked for, but I sensed a tremor of interest rippling under her skin.

"You're thinking, I bet that's the guy from Danelea,"

I said. "Me too! What can he want to see Mom for, do you suppose?"

Marnie couldn't say and although I was *itching* to find out I didn't spoil the cooling end of our ride by upping the pace, forcing myself to sit quietly as we took the long approach to our yard gate. The big car was nowhere to be seen but when I peered over the side hedge I saw it parked on our little-used front driveway.

"Come on, baby," I said and led Marnie into her stable. "Let me put your anti-sweat rug on and go indoors, then I'll come back and tell you what he's saying to Mom."

As soon as I'd untacked her she nuzzled my hair before pulling contentedly at her hay net as I left. I just about managed to bolt her door before my curiosity got the better of me, and I ran as fast as I could toward the house to find out the reason for our brand new neighbor's visit.

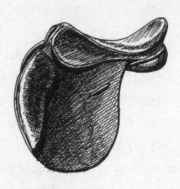

Chapter Two

As soon as I walked in I knew whatever it was, it wasn't pleasing my Mom.

"Hello darling," she greeted me, and I saw that the sparkle in her eyes was actually a glint of anger. "You're just in time to meet our new neighbor, Mr. Leyland. This is my daughter, Sian."

"We met just now," the deep voice still held that impatient note. "And my name's Christian, as I told you. And yours is –?"

"Kim," Mom said tersely. "Christian was just leaving, Sian. He has a plane to catch."

"Oh, right." I felt awkward and wished I hadn't come barging in, the atmosphere was so tense. "Um, maybe we'll see you when you get back."

"Possibly. I was just putting a proposition to your mother, one I hope she'll consider while I'm away."

"No, I'm afraid not." She lifted her chin and positively glared at him. "It's completely out of the question, I'm afraid."

With her eyes flashing and her cheeks flushed she looked quite pretty apart from the smear of paint across her top lip, I thought.

"Sian is obviously a keen equestrian. Maybe you can discuss it with her?" Christian suggested smoothly.

"If it's to do with horses I'd like to hear it." I ignored the dirty look Mom gave me.

"Mr. Leyland – Christian – wants to buy some of our land," she said sharply.

"What land?" I looked at her.

"Those two big fields alongside Danelea's boundary."

"But we need those for our winter grazing," I objected immediately.

"Exactly." She curved her mouth into a smile that didn't reach her eyes. "That's exactly what I've been telling Mr. Leyland."

"Christian," he said again. "Perhaps if you knew what I want it for, Sian – it's to build a cross country course. My daughter, Jess, is a talented rider and wants to compete. I thought having her own set-up would be an advantage."

"She's welcome to use the one I've made," I said eagerly, *really* interested now. "It's up in the woods and –"

"Oh?" he interrupted with a frown. "I was intending to get Jasper Caxton to build Jess's – he's one of the country's top course designers, as I'm sure you know."

"Sorry, I haven't heard of him." I had a brief mental picture of the very homemade and somewhat rickety set of jumps Marnie and I had constructed. "Mine aren't up to that sort of standard, but they'll give Jess and her horse some practice."

"Mm." He didn't sound convinced. "I'll let Jess know, but in the meantime if you'd give some thought to my proposition –"

"Out of the question, I'm afraid." Mom gave another of those tight-lipped smiles. "We've both told you that we need that land for our animals."

"You appear to have rather a lot of them." Christian raised his eyebrows. "I noticed five more horses out there, and your house seems full of dogs."

"And cats," I put in helpfully. "Only they're all pretty wary of strangers so they're probably keeping out of your way in the breezeway."

He blinked. "Why so many? You can only ride one horse and pat one pet at a time, surely."

"They're rescued –" I started to explain.

"And this is now their home," Mom said briskly. "So as you can see, we need all the land we have, Mr. – er – Christian."

"I'll be willing to pay a very good price –" He just wasn't getting the message.

"It's not a question of *money*," Mom interrupted impatiently. "If it was money I was interested in, I wouldn't be spending every penny I earn looking after these poor, abused creatures."

"I find your attitude odd." Christian extended a well-kept hand and shook her painted one. "It's very commendable, of course, but I think you'll find that in the end everything comes down to money; everything has its price."

19

"Not this time." Her eyes were glittering again. "The land is for our animals and is not, I repeat *not,* for sale."

"Oh well," he said and picked up his car keys. "Thank you for listening. I'd better go. It's a long drive to the airport."

"Sian will see you out." Mom turned her back and walked to her drawing board. "I must get back to my work."

I noticed Christian carefully dusting off his immaculate suit before getting into the car, and I suppressed a grin. His clothes were probably covered in cat hair from the chair and Rusty, our oldest dog, had brushed past him in the hall, no doubt leaving evidence of his own graying coat on the expensive pants. After I watched his car disappear from view I returned to Mom's studio. She's an illustrator, a really talented and gifted one, and was currently working on a children's story about a talking sheep. The sheep, with a knowing, almost human expression on its silly sheep face, was looking at me from the drawing board.

"Grr." Mom picked up a brush and dabbed it fiercely. "What an awful, horrible, arrogant man!"

"Who?" I said innocently.

"What do you mean, who?" She threw the brush down and glared at me.

"I was joking," I said. "Christian does seem a bit, well, pushy, I guess."

"Pushy!" She wiped her hand across her face, adding a blue smear to the green one already there. "He talked to me as if I was some sort of eccentric freak!"

"You probably look – unusual – to someone who's never met you before," I said, trying to be tactful.

"In what way?"

"Well, you had a dog lying on each foot, paint on your face, half that hayrack in your hair – oh, and you've tied it up with what looks like a sock."

"Oh." Her hands flew to her thick blonde mop. "It was falling in my eyes so I grabbed the first thing I found."

"Which was my sock," I said helpfully. "A bright blue one with a pink toe and heel. Very attractive."

"Ah, who cares?" She tore it out and shook her hair loose. "It doesn't matter in the least if *Christian* Leyland thinks I'm some sort of scruffy nutcase. With a little luck I'll never need to see him again."

"Mm." I wasn't so sure. "I'd like to meet his daughter, though. I wonder how old she is? Grown up,

I guess, if he's leaving her home on her own. Or is her mom staying too?"

"There's no mom; Jess is being looked after by the housekeeper and her husband. And she's thirteen, same as you."

"Excellent," I said cheerfully. "I'll go and say hello tomorrow, OK?"

"She'll probably be a nightmare." Mom was determined to be negative about our new neighbors. "With a father like Christian, how can she be anything else?"

But as it turned out she couldn't have been more wrong. Despite her misgivings I was eager to have a horse riding buddy living so close, so Marnie and I visited Danelea the next morning, and it was Jess who greeted us.

"Hi!" Her small, elfin face lit up when she saw us. "Isn't your pony *beautiful*!"

I liked her immediately.

"Thanks. Her name's Marnie and I'm Sian. We're from Greylodge, next door. You must be Jess."

"How did you know? Oh, my dad! He said he was going to call on you before he went to the airport."

"Yes, he did." I diplomatically avoided mentioning we

hadn't liked the reason for his visit. "He says you ride, too."

"Yes," she said, beaming proudly. "And now that we've moved here I finally have my own pony. I've spent five years at an equestrian center riding their horses and I still can't believe Tag is mine. Do you want to see him?"

"Please." I slid off Marnie's back and walked with Jess to the small yard a short way from the house.

Marnie, as she always does, followed, her soft nose just touching the back of my arm.

"You're not holding onto her!" Jess's eyes shone. "How awesome is that!"

"She's known me since she was just a few hours old," I explained. "And we've been this close ever since."

"Wow," Jess breathed. "I really, *really* hope Tag will get to feel that way about me. He only arrived yesterday and he's kind of jumpy."

"It's very unsettling for a horse, coming to a new home, even if it's a good one," I said sagely. "He'll soon settle down. What other horses are there here?"

"There aren't," she said, looking surprised. "Dad doesn't ride and neither do Madge or Jimmy."

Poor old Tag, I thought, my heart going out to him.

All on his own in a strange new world. Aloud I said cheerfully, "Well he'll certainly be pleased to see Marnie, in that case."

Tag, a handsome, well-bred dark bay, was looking over the door of his stable and he let out a long, high-pitched whinny as he watched us approach. Marnie whickered back agreeably and moved close to touch noses with him.

"You're right! He likes her!" Jess beamed and slid her arm around her pony's neck. "Would you two like to join us for a ride in our ring? Dad had it made for me when he was getting the house refurbished. It's great and –"

"Um, I actually promised Marnie a trail ride," I said apologetically. "Up till today we've been stuck in our own ring because of the weather. We're OK with doing schooling, obviously, but it's more fun out in the open. She and I have made a sort of cross-country course – you and Tag can come with us and have a ride around it if you'd like."

"Oh I *like*," she clapped her hands enthusiastically. "And I'm sure Tag will too."

She rushed off to get her saddle and bridle and started tacking up while we watched over the stable door. She seemed a little clumsy and I saw the bay pony's ears go back when she practically dropped the saddle in place.

"Um – it might be better to slide it carefully onto the numnah," I suggested diffidently. "Tag's back is probably cold, so that way it won't be a shock to his system."

"Sorry, my baby." she scratched gently behind her horse's ears. "I'm not very good at this, am I? I promise I'll get better."

"Didn't the equestrian center give you much practice at tacking up?" I asked and she shook her head.

"Not really. Mostly I just turned up and climbed aboard whichever horse they'd allocated. I'm pretty bad at stable management too. It took me forever to muck out this morning."

I was staggered. To me, being able to care for your horse is every bit as important as learning to ride correctly, and I said so.

She looked apologetic. "The center *did* run courses on all aspects of horse care but my dad said I should stick to riding. He didn't see the sense in paying them for the privilege of cleaning up their horses."

I opened my mouth to say just how stupid I thought that was, but then closed it again. It wasn't Jess's fault her father held such an arrogant viewpoint and she was obviously trying her hardest to look after Tag properly. I just hoped she could at least ride well and that I wouldn't be spending my morning picking her up off the woodland floor or chasing a runaway Tag she'd failed to control. As she moved the bay pony to follow Marnie and me onto the trail outside, I figured slightly grimly that it wasn't going to be long before I found out!

Chapter Three

After only the first few minutes I was pretty sure that it was going to be all right. Jess was a good rider, sitting lightly without fidgeting and keeping a soft but positive contact through her reins to the bit. Tag moved beautifully at walk, striding confidently in the four-time beat as its rhythm flowed through the muscles of his hindquarters over his back, shoulders and neck. I've heard Mom say you can tell a lot from the way a horse walks and I could see what she meant. Tag was a real athlete, supple and powerful, and Jess was perfectly attuned to his every movement.

She also understood the importance of warming our horses up before we increased the pace, and kept Tag under perfect control even when he tried to dance away as his hooves touched the invitingly springy turf leading up to the woods. She was good company too and we chatted happily, pausing only to admire a particular view or watch with pleasure as a herd of deer trotted gracefully across a nearby field.

"It's fabulous here." Jess's eyes were shining. "Dad didn't tell me we were moving until everything was signed, and since I've only lived in the city I was a little worried I wouldn't like it here."

"But you do?" I glanced at her beaming face. "Yeah, I can see you do."

"It's great," Jess said. She bent low and gave Tag's neck a hug. "The house is nice, the stables are nice and the countryside is *amazing*. Tag and I are going to have the time of our lives here."

Her face was certainly alive with happiness and after we'd trotted, then cantered along the gentle slope leading to the woods, I turned in my saddle to smile back at her.

"Do you want to try some cross-country? Not exactly competition standard, I'm afraid, but the jumps are fun and you'll see what Tag can do."

"Great," she gently brought a prancing Tag back to her hands. "My pony is so full of energy, he's going to love this."

"Let's do it properly." I was thinking that her dad said she was eager to compete. "We'll walk the course, well, ride it at walk actually, so you can see the route I planned out and the type of thing you'll be jumping."

Tag was so excited at the sight of our makeshift fences he again started dancing and jogging on the spot, swaying like a real-life rocking horse and transmitting his exuberance to Marnie, whose skin rippled as she fizzed with anticipation.

"I think I'd better go before she explodes like a rocket," I laughed. "See you at the finish line, Jess!"

Marnie, her good manners and training suppressing any tendency to charge heedlessly away, struck off on the correct leg and approached the first "fence" – in fact a line of close-packed bushes – in the smooth three-time rhythm of a canter. I sat perfectly still and balanced, leaving her unhampered to clear the jump comfortably and to land faultlessly, turning slightly in the air so she was pointing toward jump number two, a natural ditch. Her favorite fence, the substantial one we'd made using a fallen log with criss-crossed trees against it, was number nine in the sequence and she soared confidently over it. I knew everything was perfect: cadence, balance, contact and unity. Three smaller fences and we were done, galloping through the "finish line" – actually a wide space between two chestnut trees – with a triumphant flourish.

"Well *done,* Marnie." I hugged her neck and patted her extravagantly. "Come on, let's move over to that ledge so we can watch how well our new friends do."

Jess and Tag were very impressive, in fact, handling the varied course well with only a tendency to rush the simpler fences marring an otherwise perfect performance.

"Brilliant!" The smile and praise I gave them were genuine. "No one would ever know you two have only just gotten together – you make a terrific partnership."

"Thanks, Sian." Jess's cheeks glowed and her eyes shone with happiness. "That's just how it feels, and I already love Tag to bits."

"And I bet he's starting to feel the same way about

you," I said. "He obviously trusts you and likes that you're firm but kind."

"I just wish I knew more about looking after him." her face clouded a little. "I'm pretty confident when it comes to riding and I've got all his diet and everything written down, but I don't know much about the everyday stuff."

"You soon will," I promised. "Anyway, you've always got me and my mom to ask if you're not sure. We've been caring for horses – well, forever, really."

"Yeah?" She looked at me. "And your dad too?"

"He died." I didn't look back at her when I said it, because I don't like the way people's faces change when I tell them.

They usually don't know what to say so they change the subject completely or, much worse, ask tons of questions. Jess didn't do either.

She said. "That's sad. I don't have a mom; she just left us and Dad divorced her. Some of my friends feel sorry for me, but it's OK. Dad's great and so are Madge and Jimmy."

"Your housekeepers?" I didn't mention I'd felt sympathy for her that her father had flown off somewhere, leaving her with the staff.

"Yeah, I've known them since I was tiny. Madge is beautiful, and Jimmy makes you laugh all the time. Dad says I'm as close to them as family, and that's how it feels."

"Nice," I said simply. "Will they help you with Tag?"

"Jimmy will," she said, grinning at the thought of him. "He can do just about anything and he says he's always wanted to live in the country."

"They sound great." I did a few dressage steps with Marnie to help her concentrate. "Shall we try the course the other way around now? It means a couple of the jumps will have a slight downhill approach, so –"

"So I'll have to make sure Tag's weight doesn't fall on his forehand by using my legs and hands to keep him together," she said and grinned at me. "Don't worry, Sian, I know how to ride, and I want Tag to enjoy everything we do together."

"OK." I smiled back. "I'll save my lectures for stable and field management, then."

"I'm going to need all the help I can get," she said. She sat quietly and relaxed her hands to settle her still excited pony. "But *this* I can do! Can Tag and I go around the course first this time?"

"Sure." I kept Marnie moving to keep her muscles

warm and watched Jess and her horse soar confidently over the jumps in reverse order.

I thoroughly enjoyed the morning and as we rode gently back toward Danelea, I could see how much Jess had too.

"That was great – totally great!" She stopped beaming and frowned in concentration. "Now, when I get Tag back to his stable, I have to untack him, get any mud and sweat off, and then cover him with a light rug, right?"

"Yes. Of course, if you're not going to ride him again, or not till the evening, say, he'd be better off being turned out."

"Out him in the field, you mean?" She made a worried face. "What if I can't catch him again?"

"Of course you will." I stared at her. "I – oh, I suppose you've never tried."

"Not with Tag or any other horse," she admitted. "Can't he just live in his stable?"

"He'll be bored out of his skull," I said, "and full of unreleased energy and pent-up frustration which could make him dangerous to ride. Anyway, horses prefer living outdoors and you want him to be happy, don't you?"

"Of course I do. More than anything," she sighed deeply. "I've got an awful lot to learn, haven't I?"

"You'll be fine," I assured her. "There are tons of books on care and nutrition and you've got us – me and my mom. Most of what you need comes down to common sense anyway."

"Let's just hope I've got some of that, then." Jess smiled and relaxed again. "Hey, where are you taking us?"

I was moving Marnie toward the spot in the riverbank where it shelved gently into the water.

"Let's see how Tag feels about getting his feet wet."

The bay pony was very curious, lowering his head to sniff at the clear water swirling softly around his hooves. Marnie loves a dip and will happily swim in the deeper water further out, but today was just Tag's introduction to this new element so I kept her in the shallows. Tag and Jess followed us slowly until the river reached above his knees. He raised his off-fore hoof and brought it down sharply, making Jess laugh.

"Look – he's splashing Marnie!"

"Be careful," I warned. "He might want to roll; some horses love to do that in water."

"Oooh," she shrieked as her pony pawed energetically at the surface of the river again. "I think you're right, he's trying to lie down!"

"Ask him to go forward instead." I moved Marnie further along and Jess, still wide-eyed, got Tag to follow.

"At least he's not scared of water." I couldn't help giggling at the expression on her face. "It takes forever to get some ponies swimming."

"Swimming?" she breathed. "Oh that would be *fantastic*. Can we –?"

"Not today." I turned my beautiful pony toward the bank. "For one thing we'd ruin their saddles and get our clothes soaked. Maybe in a day or two."

"Great." She smiled blissfully. "Riding at the equestrian center was never like this."

I liked her enthusiasm, the way she laughed and chatted, everything about her really, and by the time we rode back along Danelea's immaculate drive I knew I'd found a friend.

"OK." Jess dismounted and ran her stirrups efficiently up their leathers. "This has always been the point where I hand the horse over to a groom, so I guess you'd better tell me again what to do now that I'm in the real world."

I grinned and slid to the ground. "Untack, put a head collar on and tie him up, then check him over and brush him down. Then lead him to his field, assuming you've already made sure the fencing is safe and he's got plenty of clean water."

"We did that earlier this morning," said a slightly worried-looking man as he came out of a stable. "And Jess asked me to make sure everything in the stables was safe as well."

"Hello Jimmy." Jess beamed at him. "We had a *terrific* ride."

"You look happy." he smiled fondly back. "Did your horse behave himself all right?"

"Your horse," she repeated dreamily. "I still can't get used to it."

"Better hurry up, then," he joked. "Your dad wants you winning cups by the end of the summer."

"Maybe they will be," I said. "Jess is a good rider and Tag's a beautiful horse."

"So all we have to do is *keep* him beautiful." Jimmy stretched out his hand and shook mine. "You must be the young lady from next door."

"Yes, she's Sian and she knows *everything*." Jess was busily stripping off Tag's saddle and bridle. "And Sian and her mom will help us –"

"Look out," I said hurriedly. "You haven't put a head collar on Tag and he's wandering off."

Jess dumped the saddle on the ground and went after him, just managing to slide an arm around his neck before he left the yard. I spent the next twenty minutes showing her how to tie him with a quick-release knot to a ring in the wall and got her checking him thoroughly, picking his feet out, brushing him down and offering him a drink. Then Marnie and I walked with them to the field that adjoined the stable yard.

"How long will it be before Tag follows me the way your pony does?" Jess had a million questions.

"He might never do it; most ponies don't. We're a bit special because we've always been together. Marnie's mother came to us from a rescue center who didn't know her history or that she was in foal. I was only eight when Marnie was born so we've sort of grown up together."

"What happened to the rescued mare – her mom?"

"She's back at Greylodge with our others. Her name's Gail," I said. "Make Tag stand at your shoulder while you undo the gate and teach him to stay there when you turn and close it again."

"OK," she said, looking anxious at the thought of releasing him. "Here we go, Tag – freedom!"

Chapter Four

For a moment the bay pony stood absolutely still. Then he moved forward in a beautiful extended trot that quickly became a canter, his black mane and tail streaming in the wind. Muscles rippling, he flew across the grass, now swerving, arching and bucking for sheer joy.

"He is so beautiful." There were tears in Jess's eyes as she watched her horse. "And so clever – look, Sian, a flying leg change, oh and a pirouette – I didn't even know he could *do* that!"

"It's all natural movement." I was touched by the emotion on her face. "It's amazing what horses are capable of. The trick is learning how to ask them."

"What's he doing now? Look, he's pawing at the ground the way he did in the river."

Tag had stopped cavorting and was now picking a spot in the field to roll. He turned around several times but just as I thought he'd drop to the ground he changed his mind and moved away again. This time, after a few minutes of pawing and circling, he collapsed with a grunt of satisfaction, squirming his back into the ground as his neat hooves waved comically in the air.

"Now he's happy," I grinned at Jess and hopped back aboard the patiently waiting Marnie. "I'd better take my girl home so she can do the same."

"I'll just stay here and watch Tag for a while," Jess smiled at me without taking her eyes off her pony. "Can I call you if I can't catch him or he won't eat or –"

"You can call me about *anything*." We'd already swapped phone numbers. "But don't worry, you're going to be fine."

As I rode away I waved to Jimmy and his tiny, friendly-looking wife, Madge, who both waved madly back. I was singing when I got to Greylodge and still humming happily as I opened the gate for Marnie to rejoin her friends in the field. She always trotted over to say hello before indulging in a nice roll, and I felt sad for Tag that he didn't have a companion to share his lovely new home.

"So, how was it? Is Jess OK? Or is she a spoiled brat?" Mom was looking neater today, her hair held back in a proper band and she wasn't covered in paint or hay.

"Not a brat at all," I said. "Really, *really* nice."

"And as good a rider as her father claims?"

"Yeah, she's terrific, only –" I hesitated.

"Only what? Oh, don't tell me all she wants to do is win competitions and she's already working on you to make me sell them our land!"

"Calm down," I said, sounding, as I often do, like I'm the grown-up and she's the kid. "Jess didn't even mention buying our fields and she seemed to love the jumping course in the woods."

"Oh." Mom gave this some thought. "What did she say about Christian coming over here, then?"

I shrugged. "Not much. I don't think she knows the reason – she certainly didn't seem hung up on competing anyhow."

"But her dad says he paid a lot of money for a top horse," she objected. "So –"

"Tag's gorgeous," I agreed. "And probably capable of winning stuff, but Jess just wants to get to know him and love him."

"That's really good," she said, her voice changing immediately. "She sounds just like you, Sian. Maybe you've found a soul mate!"

"I don't know about that," I said cautiously. "But, yeah, I like her and you will too. I said we'd help her with Tag."

"Help her? I thought you said she didn't need help with her riding."

"Not with that," I looked at her. "Jess doesn't have a clue how to look after him. She's never had her own horse before, just lots of lessons at an equestrian center."

"No!" Mom sat down on the bench in our yard. "Does she have a groom?"

"No, just Jimmy. He and Madge look after everything, including Jess, when her dad goes away on business."

"Poor little girl," she exploded. "I knew that Christian Leyland was an insensitive, uncaring man, but to dump his own daughter –"

"Will you calm down!" I ordered again. "I've never known you to get so steamed up about a person before."

I went on to explain about Jess's background, the divorce, the fact that she loved Jimmy and Madge and the fact that they'd all lived only in a city apartment before.

"So Jimmy doesn't know anything about horse care either?" She was quieter now but still shocked. "We'll have to keep a close eye on Tag, Sian, to make sure he's properly fed and happy."

"I think Jess will be fine. She already loves Tag and is learning everything she can about looking after him, and Jimmy's eager to help her. The worst thing," I said, hesitating, "is that Tag is on his own. There are no other horses at Danelea."

"That doesn't surprise me," she said fiercely. "It would never occur to someone like Christian that horses need company. Did you explain that to Jess?"

"Not really. There's so much she has to take in and I didn't want to worry her when there's nothing she can do about it while her dad's away."

"That's true. As soon as he gets back, though, Christian must be told he needs to get another horse."

42

She got up and started walking toward the house. "Now, could you give me a hand with Rusty? His claws are a bit long and you know he doesn't like me trimming them unless you're cuddling him."

Our dogs get plenty of exercise, which wears their claws down naturally, but Rusty has always had a problem with his. When he first came to us they were so long he could barely walk and he still doesn't like having them clipped. I sat on the floor with him and hugged him close, singing quietly to distract him and feeding him tiny bits of his favorite cheese. He loved it and stayed very still so Mom could trim each paw quickly, with Rusty giving an occasional thump of his tail to show his approval of our nail-trimming system.

"There." Mom put the clippers away and gave the old dog a warm hug. "That'll do, Rusty. Good boy. You were excellent, and so were you, Sian."

"Gee, thanks," I teased. "That's another skill I can put on my résumé."

"You've got quite a lot, haven't you?" She grinned back. "So, would you mind helping me with a few more? It's nearly feeding time."

"Sure." I gave Rusty the last bit of cheese and got up.

43

There was always plenty to do around the place, but I enjoyed being part of it all.

"What's Jess doing with the rest of her day?" Mom asked as we sorted out the food. "Now that summer vacation is here she can always come on over if she's lonely."

"She said she was going to school Tag later – that is, if she can catch him." I grinned at the thought. "It seems weird she knows so much about riding, yet virtually nothing about the practical stuff."

"I think it's a disgrace." Mom sniffed and stirred the hens' pots vigorously. "On her father's part, I mean. What sort of man buys his young daughter a horse without either of them having the faintest idea how to look after it?"

"The sort who thinks because Jess has spent so much time with horses she must know everything, I guess." I didn't want her going off on a rant. "Jess says her dad is great and was thrilled to bits about getting Tag for her."

"Not great enough to learn stable management or get company for the poor horse," she said, snorting.

"Yeah, OK, he should have gotten advice on that." I took the chicken feed away before she stirred it into mush. "But the main thing is Jess loves Tag and we're here to help, so everything will be fine."

"No thanks to Christian Leyland." She pushed her bangs crossly out of her eyes.

"Now you've got corn in your hair," I told her. "Whenever you start talking about him you end up looking like a scarecrow!"

"Don't be cheeky," she said, pretending to threaten me with a spoon. "And yes, you're right, with a bit of help Tag *will* be well cared for, but I still wish he had company."

"You can work on Christian when he gets back," I said. "Jess is going to tell him about it too so he won't stand a chance of refusing."

"It's not my place to tell him what to do," she said huffily. "I don't want anything to do with him anyway."

"OK." I picked up some feeds and walked out into the sunshine. "Just forget it, then."

I kept strictly off the subject for the rest of the day as the mere mention of Christian's name seemed to rile my mom up so much. She's usually pretty placid, pottering around her beloved animals or working in her studio, but the new neighbor had gotten under her skin and made her pretty cranky. The time passed in its usual peaceful yet busy way and I loved the thought of the vacation weeks stretching before me. I did a little schooling on Marnie and we spent a lazy hour afterwards just wandering around the field together. She'd already accompanied me when I'd cleaned it earlier and Mom, who saw us, said she almost expected my pony to pick up a shovel or a wheelbarrow to help! I loved the fact that Marnie and I were so close and hoped Jess was starting to feel the same connection with her beautiful new boy. The answer to that came pretty early the next morning and it wasn't the positive one I was expecting.

"Sian!" Jess was on the phone and she sounded upset. "I don't know what to do!"

"What's the matter?" I tucked the phone under my chin and let the chickens out of their coop. "Can't you catch Tag?"

"It's not that. He was as good as gold yesterday. He came over to me when I called and I did what you said, caught him and just petted him."

"That's good." I made sure the hens had plenty of water. "So what happened –"

"And later I caught him again and schooled him, just a short session like you said, and I remembered to put his head collar on and turn him at the gate and –"

46

"So what's wrong?" I interrupted before she could give me a complete breakdown of every minute.

"I don't know," she wailed. "I ran down to his field this morning and thought he'd be grazing, but he's not. He's sort of marching up and down along the fence and he's whinnying – listen!"

She held her phone out and I could hear Tag in the background.

"He's not hurt?" I asked worriedly. "Injured himself, or –"

"No, I don't think so. I've checked and checked him."

"Talk to him very soothingly, put him in his stable and stay with him," I said. "I've just got the ducks to feed and then I'll saddle Marnie and come over. OK?"

"OK." She gave a small sob. "Thanks, Sian."

I decided against telling Mom. Tag didn't sound sick and if he looked it I'd call a vet, so I figured it was better to find out more before telling her.

"She's so prejudiced against Christian she'd overreact," I told Marnie, who seemed very pleased to be going out so early. "Let's take a look first."

It was another lovely day and the short ride to Danelea was full of bird song and dappled sunshine. Marnie stepped out joyfully, but when I saw her ears begin to flicker rapidly I knew something was wrong. A few moments later my less sensitive hearing caught it too – a series of high-pitched whinnying cries coming from the stable yard we were now approaching.

Chapter Five

"Poor Tag," I murmured. "Call back to him, Marnie; tell him we're coming."

She made a long, low, whickering sound that sounded, even to human ears, warm and comforting. Tag's response was immediate and sounded less strident than before, but I could also hear him kicking hard against the stable door in his anxiety to see us. As we entered the yard the bay horse nodded his head up and down vigorously and kept on kicking, but the shrill whinny had softened.

"It's OK, Tag." I slid off Marnie's back and walked alongside her to his stable. "Marnie's here. Tell her what's bothering you."

My pony put her pretty nose against his and blew gently. Tag stopped his anxious kicking, relaxed his neck and nuzzled against her.

"Oh, wow." The tension flowed out of Jess too. "That's amazing – I haven't been able to calm him at all."

"What set him off, do you know?" I quietly reached up a hand and stroked the bay pony's ears. "He sounded pretty distressed."

"I don't know," she said and shook her head tearfully. "He seemed to settle really well, just kept grazing after you left yesterday, and as I told you, he was good as gold to catch."

Jimmy stopped filling a hay net and came over to join us.

"After you rode him – schooled him, I think you call it – and then put him back in his field he went around and around it several times, I noticed."

"Well yeah, but he did that when I first turned him out, didn't he, Sian?" Jess turned to me. "It was great to watch him galloping free and then rolling so happily."

"Yes it was," I agreed. "But maybe the second time,

50

after you'd worked with him, he realized this is it, he's all on his own. I think he was pacing up and down looking for his friends. That's probably why he keeps calling."

"No way!" Jimmy said incredulously. "It can't be that – he's just a horse. As long as they're well looked after and have plenty to eat they're fine, surely?"

"My mom wouldn't agree with that," I said darkly. "I know some horses get used to being on their own, but she says they're naturally herd animals and they should always have company."

"Well." Jimmy scratched his head. "I don't know what your dad will think about that, Jess."

"We'll soon find out." Jess's small face had a very determined expression on it. "I'm going to call him right now."

"Now?" I said. "Wouldn't it be better to talk about it when he comes home?"

"He's at a business conference the whole week." Jess had already started walking toward the house. "Tag will be out of his mind with worry by then."

"I don't think it's a good idea to call your dad when he's working." Jimmy patted Tag kindly. "Why not wait till tonight when he calls you from his hotel?"

"No." She didn't turn her head. "I'm doing it now. I'll have to use the house phone."

"You – uh – might make him mad by calling now." I could imagine Christian's reaction if his conference was interrupted because of an upset pony. "Look, Marnie can spend the day here with Tag to help him quiet down, then you can –um – discuss buying another horse for company when your dad calls to say hello."

She stopped and turned on her heel. "It's really kind of you and yeah, I'd love Marnie to stay with Tag, but it's only a temporary solution isn't it? Dad needs to sort out something permanent and he needs to do it right away."

I heard Jimmy suppress a sigh and realized he'd seen this assertive side of Jess's nature before.

"Don't worry." He smiled at me as Jess disappeared from view. "Jess's dad will do anything for her. I'm betting there'll be another pony at Danelea before Christian even gets back!"

I kept on gently scratching Tag's neck while he and Marnie continued nuzzling and inhaling each other's scent. Jess was gone for quite a while, but when she returned I could see right away her phone call hadn't gone well.

"He wouldn't talk about another horse." She pressed her lips together. "I called his cell but it was switched off so I phoned the conference center and they went and got him."

"Jess, you shouldn't have done that," Jimmy said crossly. "Your poor dad must have thought there was a real emergency."

"Well there is," she shook her head defiantly. "Only you're right, Dad didn't think so. He came rushing to the phone but when I told him about Tag he got mad. He was just about to start a presentation or something when they called him to reception."

"Uh-oh," I stopped stroking Tag. "I'm guessing you're in deep trouble now."

She gave another couldn't-care-less toss of her head. "He said he'd been terrified the phone call was Jimmy saying I'd been injured riding, but when I told him the problem was just as serious he practically slammed the phone down on me."

"Not a good way to ask him for another horse." I looked at her. "So what are you going to do now?"

"I'd better not call again," she said and chewed her bottom lip. "I'll just have to explain it better when he calls tonight. Can Marnie stay here for a while, like you said?"

"Sure," I said. "I've helped with all the morning chores at home. Mom knows I've gone out for a ride so maybe I could show you and Tag around again, then Marnie can keep him company in his field when we get back."

"Do you think he's safe for Jess to ride while he's in this mood?" Poor Jimmy was struggling with this new aspect of their lives.

"I'm sure he is. He's a properly trained, well schooled horse and Jess knows what she's doing."

"Yeah I'm all right once I'm in the saddle," Jess said gloomily. "Just completely useless about how to make him happy when I'm not."

"Duh!" I laughed at her frowning face. "You haven't had him forty eight hours yet – you'll get it right."

"Maybe you should stay here and do some more of that schooling." Jimmy was still worrying.

"But I want to go out with Sian and Marnie." Jess was beginning to sound like the spoiled brat my mom had mentioned, but then I saw her eyes soften when she looked at him."Well, OK. I don't want you to worry, Jimmy. How about if we spend some time in the school before we go out? That way you can see how well behaved Tag is."

"Good idea," I said heartily. "Get him tacked up then, Jess, and we'll do some warming up."

I was expecting something similar to the ring at Greylodge, a roped-off area behind the stables with home-made markers and a few oil drums and poles for jumping practice, so when I followed Jess into a professional ring with post and rail fencing, top grade surfacing and proper colored jumps and dressage markers, I was totally blown away.

"Wow." I blinked. "Your dad sure takes your riding seriously, doesn't he?"

It was her turn to look surprised. "Yeah, I guess. I said I needed somewhere to school my new horse so he had this built. You've got one as well, haven't you?"

I thought of the bits of string and traffic cones we'd used and grinned. "Not on this scale!"

"Oh well," she said and moved Tag forward. "You're welcome to use this any time you like."

Jimmy sat on the top bar of the fence and watched intently as we put our ponies through a series of warm ups and a little lateral work.

"Tag's a completely different horse now." He was beaming with relief when we finished. "He's doing everything you ask him."

"Like I said, I know what I'm doing once I'm riding." Jess smiled back at him. "So don't worry Jimmy, I'll be fine when we go out."

"OK, but make sure you've got your cell phone with you."

"It's here," she said, fishing it out of her pocket, "but it keeps sort of breaking up when I try to call out. Maybe I need a new one."

"It won't make any difference," I told her. "This valley has really poor reception – something to do with the hills blocking the signal."

"That's all I need." Jimmy's face creased with anxiety again. "You not being able to call if you need me!"

"It'll be OK," I reassured him. "It's just a little patchy, that's all."

"Off you go then, I suppose." He didn't want to spoil our fun. "But *be careful*."

"Yes Jimmy, certainly Jimmy." Jess grinned cheekily at him. "I promise, honest."

She moved Tag to walk alongside Marnie as we made our way along the driveway to the big gates.

"Do you want another go around the cross-country course?" I asked. "Or shall I show you another route that's got a great galloping trail – it might help Tag to relax if he can let off a bit of steam."

"That sounds great," she said, her eyes shining at the thought. "And maybe we could swim after."

"We haven't got towels and stuff," I said, being practical as always. "We'll do that later in the week, maybe."

I thought she might object. She was obviously a girl used to getting her own way, but she didn't argue.

"Whatever you think, Sian. If it makes Tag happy, then I'm happy too."

We had a great ride and the bay horse really did seem to enjoy himself. He got very excited when we reached the long sloping incline of the galloping trail and I thought for a moment he was going to get away from Jess, but she handled him well, bringing him back to her hands and not allowing him to bolt mindlessly.

"He seems to like to race." She laughed as the soft wind whipped color into her cheeks.

"Most horses do." I smiled back at her. "It's perfectly natural and a lot of fun, as long as you stay in control."

"Tag pulls a bit," she said and eased him down to a collected canter, "but he listens to me when I ask him not to."

"You ride him really well," I said genuinely. "Your dad could be right about you two winning lots of competitions."

"Maybe." She patted her pony's shoulder. "But that's way down the list of things to do. First of all I have to make sure Tag's happy, and that means –"

"Yeah I know." I thought it best to stay off the subject, since she got so heated about it. "Getting him company. Come on, I'll show you the part of the river I like best for swimming in. It's just along here."

The trail leading to the wide, safe expanse of water is a narrow, twisting one so we slowed from trot down to walk, ducking our heads to avoid the low branches of the trees that line it.

I heard Jess gasp when we reached the riverbank, and smiled. "It's nice, isn't it?"

"Nice? *Nice?*" Her eyes were wide. "It's – it's – *sensational!* Wait till I tell Dad!"

The river is always lovely but this, my favorite spot, is particularly so and I was glad city girl Jess was impressed by it. A shimmering stretch of gently flowing water gleamed before us, fringed by willow trees that trailed long fingers into their own graceful reflections. The grassy bank shelved gradually into the river's shallows where tiny fish darted among the water's silver ripples.

"Can't we go in?" Jess turned imploring eyes on me. "To swim, I mean?"

I shook my head firmly. "We can paddle again if you want, but we need to bring swim suits or shorts plus lots of towels. And I think you should try riding Tag without a saddle before you actually take the plunge together."

"You're so sensible." she moaned. "Seeing this just makes me want to take off like – like a mermaid!"

"Fine, but it would ruin your saddle *and* your fancy boots." I laughed. "And you don't want to upset your dad by asking for brand new ones already."

"True." She let Tag lower his head to sniff at the water. "I'm already telling him to buy another horse, so I guess that's enough for one day!"

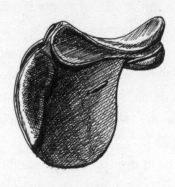

Chapter Six

I privately thought she should be *asking* but hey, the way
she speaks to her dad is none of my business, is it? Tag
and Marnie enjoyed their cooling paddle and I was sure
we'd have no trouble at all persuading the bay pony to
plunge into the deeper water further out in the river when
we were ready. I think Jess and I would have happily
stayed out all day, but hunger pangs combined with a
crackly, slightly anxious phone call from Jimmy sent us
back to Danelea for lunch. I called Mom to tell her I was

staying, and Jess, still full of smiling enthusiasm, asked Madge to fix us a picnic.

"We can eat it in the field while we watch Tag and Marnie." She finished scraping some mud off her pony. "That's if you don't mind?"

"No, that'll be great." I'd untacked Marnie and brushed her down as she stood quietly next to Tag in the yard.

"Look at her," Jess said enviously. "She's so clean she gleams, and you didn't have to tie her up or anything, did you?"

"Nope," I said proudly. "And she'll come to the field with me, too. It doesn't matter that we don't have a head collar. Are you and Tag ready?"

"Think so. Does he look all right?" She stood back and squinted at her horse.

"Not bad," I said, trying to be encouraging but honest. "Though you've missed a few spots. You'll get better the more you do it."

"I hope so," she said fervently. "The way you do Marnie makes her look *perfect*."

"That's cuz she is." I laughed and tickled my pony behind her ears. "Come on baby, you're going to keep your new friend company in his field."

Marnie tucked herself in at my shoulder and walked with

me to the field, waiting patiently while Jess sorted out the new routine of turning Tag out. She managed very well and stood looking thrilled as the two beautiful horses trotted across the grass. I thought there might be a few fireworks, a bit of showing off from Tag, but he simply followed Marnie wherever she went, only occasionally looking around him, as if a little unsure. When she decide on a suitable patch to roll in he chose one right alongside her and to Jess's delight there were *eight* legs, four bay and four dark gray, waving happily in the air. We'd spread out the excellent picnic Madge had prepared and had a great time eating, drinking and chatting as our horses settled equally amicably to some grazing. Because we'd had a pretty long ride that morning we decided to give both ponies a quiet afternoon.

"Hopefully, having Marnie with him will reassure Tag he's not going to be on his own forever," I said to Jess. "Spending a few hours with her should go a long way to keeping him calm."

"Yeah, he's completely different now." Jess looked lovingly at him across the field. "What shall we do while they're both chilling out?"

"I could show you some more stable stuff," I suggested. "Or is that too boring?"

"*Nothing* is too boring when it's for Tag." She waved her arms dramatically. "I'll do anything, absolutely *anything* for him."

"Yeah?" I said. "Including mucking out and tack cleaning?"

"Maybe not my favorites," she admitted, "but necessary. I'm pretty bad at both, so show me how they should be done."

We actually laughed a lot despite the dull chores we were doing. Jess was good company, very cheerful and also, to my surprise, extremely hard working. I made her laugh, demonstrating some of the games and songs I'd made up to help make jobs like cleaning water buckets and feed troughs a little more interesting.

"Hey!" She was copying my "polishing dance" as she worked on Tag's saddle. "This is great. It actually makes you finish the thing quicker!"

"I know, and wait till you try my broom race – I can sweep out a stable even quicker than my mom now."

"And I bet with all the horses you've got, she's pretty quick." Jess hesitated. "Have you always had rescued animals? Even before your dad died, I mean?"

"Oh yeah, it was Dad's passion, really, and at first

Mom said she stood back a little. She grew up in the city like you, so initially looking after all the horses and everything came as quite a shock."

"Yeah? And yet she can do *everything* now, can't she?"

"I suppose so." I hadn't really thought about it. "My dad taught her to ride, I know that, so I guess she must have learned all the other stuff from him too."

"That's good," she said seriously. "I was worried that to be any use I might have to be, you know, *born* into the country lifestyle like you were, but if your mom learned it all from scratch, I can too."

"Course you can." I threw my cloth down. "Look at the wonderful job you've done on Tag's saddle."

"I made a total mess of putting his bridle back together, though." She made a face. "I just couldn't work out what went where."

"You'll do better next time." I patted her head jokily. "You don't have to take it apart every time you ride, so don't worry."

"And you'll go through it again with me, won't you?"

"Sure. Like I said, you're not on your own. Mom and I will help whenever you want."

"Great." She smiled with relief. "I can't wait to meet

her *and* all your horses, dogs, cats, chickens, ducks and –
um –"

"Pigs," I said succinctly. "Don't forget the pigs."

Another dull, but essential job was to clean the field,
but when Jess saw the way Marnie accompanied me and
my wheelbarrow she was instantly enchanted.

"I want Tag to do that." She stroked Marnie's
shoulder. "Ooh look – he's coming over."

I didn't mention her horse was probably just eager
to stay close to Marnie rather than to Jess. It takes a
while to build up a relationship, but I was sure that
Jess and Tag would soon bond, and the connection
would give her the same kind of joy I had. There
wasn't a lot of cleaning to do, so once we'd tidied up
and put away the forks and wheelbarrow we just hung
out in the field and played a few silly games. Rolling
like a pony was one of them. It was Jess's idea, and
involved our trying to do a realistic impression of
our horses' ritual. Jess was easily the best at it, and
her routine of pawing in a circle, then dropping to
the ground and squirming her back into the grass
looked so funny my ribs ached from laughing. We also
climbed a big old oak in a corner of the paddock and

made the beginnings of a tree house in the center fork of its huge branches. It was nice up there; a cooling breeze lifted the leaves that completely concealed us from the ground. Scrambling around the main section of our "house," I became aware that someone was calling Jess's name. Parting the leaves, I looked across the field to where Marnie and Tag were grazing and saw Jimmy standing on the lowest gate rung, peering around and shouting for Jess.

"Jimmy wants you." I ducked back inside the cool green cave where Jess was wrapping an old sack around a branch to fashion a "chair." "Come on, we'd better go."

"Hang on." She climbed further along the branch and peeked out as I'd done. "Wait till he's gone – I want this to be a secret place."

"He'll go crazy if he doesn't find you." As usual I was the sensible one. "Poor old Jimmy. He spends most of his time worrying about you."

"It's OK, he's gone." She slithered back down and grinned wickedly at my disapproving expression. "It's just a little fun, Sian. Lighten up!"

She was right, of course; I was starting to realize I didn't have to take everything quite so seriously.

"Shouldn't we go and see what Jimmy wants, though?" I asked diffidently.

"Sure, but don't tell him where we were, OK?"

"OK." I agreed and followed her down the tree, being careful, like her, to remain hidden from the house and yard.

It took a while to complete Jess's long, complicated route back to the gate. We crouched behind shrubs and wriggled through the undergrowth of a small thicket to the side of Tag's field, before emerging, pretty scratched and tousled, at the entrance to the yard.

"There you are!" Jimmy's face was creased and wrinkled with care again. "I've been looking everywhere for you two."

"We were exploring," Jess said airily, picking bits of tree out of her hair. "Sorry, did you want us?"

"I didn't, but your dad did." He still looked worried. "He was on the phone ten minutes ago and he didn't sound too happy."

Jess looked at her watch. "He doesn't usually call this early. It doesn't matter, he's bound to call back."

"You'd better figure out what you're going to say before he does," Jimmy advised. "Your dad's pretty patient where you're concerned, but he's real mad about the way you got him dragged out of his conference."

"He'll get over it, and I already know what I'm going to say – the same as before. Tag *has* to have company."

I opened my mouth to suggest she might like to phrase it a little more tactfully when my own phone rang.

"Sian?" It was Mom. "Where are you?"

"At Danelea, I told you."

"And where's Marnie?"

"She's here as well, of course." I was surprised she even had to ask. "She's in Tag's field keeping him company."

The sigh she gave nearly blew my ear off. "For goodness' sake, what are you *thinking*? Get her out of there and come home. *Now*."

"But –"

The loud click told me she'd not only hung up but probably thrown the phone down too.

"Sounds as if there's trouble." I moved quickly to the gate and called my pony, who raised her pretty head immediately. "Here Marnie, come to me."

Before I'd even stopped speaking she was trotting, then cantering, her legs, dark against her paler dappled flanks, flying in perfect symmetry.

"Phew." Jess stared at her. "I thought Tag was easy to catch but this is *awesome*!"

I opened the gate and Marnie walked smoothly through, standing perfectly as I swiftly put her bridle and saddle in place.

"Sorry Jess, I've really got to rush. Mom sounds…" I hesitated, "as though something's wrong."

"Another chicken emergency?" She looked across at Tag, standing uncertainly near the gate. "I hope it's nothing too serious. Don't worry about us, we'll be fine."

"I'll call you later," I promised as I moved my pony swiftly along the driveway again.

From what Mom had said and the tone of her voice, I knew whatever had happened meant just one thing for me when I got home – and that was trouble. *Big* trouble!

Chapter Seven

I was right; she was waiting in the yard when I got there, pushing a brush around so hard she was raising a cloud of dust.

"Be careful, you'll wear the bristles out." I tried a weak joke to lighten the atmosphere but it didn't work.

"Do you know how I've spent the last ten minutes?" she snapped.

"Uh – counting chickens? There should be fourteen," I said. Even though I suspected my banter wasn't helping I still tried.

"No, Sian. I have been arguing with Mr. Leyland."

"Christian's here?" Still stalling, I hopped out of the saddle and started to remove it from Marnie's back.

"No, he's not *here*. He's been on the phone and he's been complaining."

I opened my mouth to make a crack about the pigs trespassing again but closed it hurriedly when I realized just how mad she was.

"Well," she said and started pacing around the yard. "Aren't you going to ask exactly what he's complaining about?"

Again I started to speak but you can't interrupt my mom when she's in full flow.

"*You* – amongst other things. *You* filling his daughter's head with the kind of sentimental nonsense you obviously learned from me and *you* taking advantage of Jess's kind nature by using Danelea's paddock for your own horse's grazing!"

"What?" I stopped unbuckling Marnie's throat lash and stared at her. "That's not how it was at all!"

"Well, obviously I realize that and that's why I've been arguing with the wretched man! He told me Jess had him called out of an important meeting just to tell

71

him Tag was unhappy and he, Christian Leyland I mean, had to buy another horse so he, Tag I mean, wouldn't be on his own. Did the man think I'd seriously believe a thirteen-year-old girl would do that?"

"Um," I said uneasily, "I think that's more or less what she did say."

"No!" Mom screeched and stood totally still.

She looked ready to explode so I said quickly, "Let me turn Marnie out and then we'll sit down and I'll tell you exactly what happened."

My pony, whose ears had gone back sharply at Mom's never-before-heard scream, nudged me gently as we walked to the summer field.

"Sorry baby," I whispered, "about the yelling and about being hauled out of one field and shoved right in another. I'll be back later to explain."

She whickered understandingly against my ear as I opened the gate, then she moved quickly to join her friends who all looked welcoming as she cantered toward them.

At least our horses are pleased to see us, I thought grouchily as I trudged to the back door of the house. *Not like someone else I could mention.*

The someone else was pouring herself a cup of coffee. "Do you want anything, Sian?"

"No thanks, Mom, Jess and I had a picnic," I said unwisely.

"A picnic? How nice. I'm sure if Mr. Leyland had known that, he'd have accused you of feeding not only your pony but yourself, at his expense."

"Don't be silly," I said, keeping my voice level. "Christian's obviously upset. He tried to call Jess back just now, but – uh – Jimmy didn't know where we were. Christian must have been fuming all day about the way Jess called him, so when he couldn't talk to her about it, he kind of took it out on you."

"And that's all right, is it?" There were two scarlet discs of anger on her cheekbones. "It's OK for him to shout at whomever he likes? Even if it's someone who had no idea what he was talking about?"

"Drink your coffee and calm down," I ordered. "And I'll try to explain exactly what happened."

The circles of high color on her cheeks gradually subsided as she listened, but when I finished by saying we'd put Marnie in Tag's field to comfort him she shook her head vehemently.

73

"*That* is never going to be the answer, is it? If Tag has to live alone then he has to get used to it. It won't help if Marnie stays an hour or two with him. In fact it will only confuse him and delay the process of rehabilitation."

"Rehabilitation? Tag's not some sort of addict!" I glared at her. "He's just lonely. I told Jess what you said about horses being herd animals and needing company and –"

"And she phoned her father while he was working and not only repeated my opinion but demanded he buy another horse immediately!" Mom glared right back. "No wonder the awful man was so – so *awful*!"

"When I told Jess what I thought the reason was for Tag's distress this morning, I didn't expect her to call her dad right away." I tried to defend myself.

"She's obviously a very spoiled child who's used to getting her father to indulge her every whim." Angrily, she poured some more coffee. "So I was right to ask what you were thinking of, Sian. You should never have repeated everything I said, and you most definitely shouldn't have put Marnie in Danelea's paddock."

"I was trying to help Tag. I was trying to help the horse." It was my turn to yell. "And OK, Jess as well.

She might be spoiled, but she loves Tag and she wants him to be happy. I thought that was what you and I wanted too – horses to be happy!"

"Oh Sian." Her voice softened so that she sounded like my mom again. "We do, of course we do. But Tag isn't being abused or neglected. He's not beaten, or half starved and in need of the sort of help we've given Gail and Texas and the others."

"But he's sad," I insisted. "*Really* sad. He was calling, and kicking at his stable –"

"I know, love, and I know you meant to help him, but instead you've succeeded in angering our new neighbor. I still think he's a most objectionable man but he's not doing anything actually wrong. Lots of horses live alone."

"And they hate it," I said sulkily. "You know they do. And Tag seems to hate it more than most."

"If Mr. Leyland was a normal, reasonable man I'd point that out, but he's *not* reasonable, so all we can do is butt out, Sian. He's impossible to talk to, and now he's made up his mind we're trying to teach what he calls our weird hippie beliefs to Jess. The only way to deal with him is to leave well alone."

"But that means Tag will stay unhappy." I was close to tears. "And Jess won't know what to do."

"I'm really sorry. Perhaps you and she will meet up sometimes when you ride out. You can talk to her then, and at least Tag will get to see Marnie once in a while."

"Huh?" I couldn't believe what I was hearing. "Meet up when we're out? Jess and I are friends. I already told her to come over here and meet you and all our animals and –"

"No, I'm afraid that can't happen." She looked genuinely sorry. "Mr. Leyland was almost vitriolic in the things he said, and I'm afraid I got rather heated too. We had quite a fight, and – well I can't allow you to go to Danelea again and I think it best that Jess doesn't come here either. This way her father can't accuse us of putting subversive ideas in her head."

"I don't even know what subversive means." I was yelling again. "Jess likes me and I like her, so we're already friends and you're always saying you wish I had friends living nearby."

"I did, I do, but not Jess. I'm sorry. Not after the way her father spoke about you."

"It's not just about that, is it?" I was so upset I wanted to lash out. "It's because *you* don't like him. You hated him from the minute you met, and you're taking it out on Jess and me."

"That's enough, Sian." She was now icily calm. "I don't want either of us to have anything to do with Christian Leyland or his – household. Is that clear?"

I shouted some more but I could see I was getting absolutely nowhere so I slammed out of the house and ran to my haven, my solace and my comfort – Marnie. She was great, as always, even when I sobbed against her neck and got her all wet.

"Sorry baby." I dabbed my eyes. "Mom hardly ever makes me cry but she's being impossible this time, Marnie, and it's not fair!"

My pony curved her neck around me as though she was hugging me close, and I breathed in her sweet smell and felt better.

"What should I do?" I asked as we walked slowly across the grass together. "About Jess, I mean? I promised her we'd help with Tag if she needed us, but now I'm not allowed to go to Danelea and she can't come here in case it upsets her dad."

Marnie blew thoughtfully down her nose and I looked at her.

"That's a good idea. Jess and I can arrange to meet by the river or somewhere, can't we? Her dad and my mom can think we just happened to bump into each other – that's brilliant, Marnie!"

She nuzzled my hair happily, pleased that I was pleased.

"OK." I felt in my pocket. "I'd better call Jess before she turns up here. She won't have any idea my mom's practically banned us from getting together so –"

As I pulled out my cell it started to ring – and what do you know, it was Jess.

"Hi," she said breathlessly. "I thought I'd better call. I've got a problem."

"With Tag?" My heart sank.

"No, well a bit, but not too bad. He's mostly grazing, just lifts his head every now and then and sort of calls out. No, it's my dad."

"Oh?" I guessed what was coming.

"Yeah. He's – uh – well, he's – uh –"

"Banned me from coming to Danelea," I said. "And told you you're not to call me."

"How did you – oh, did he tell your mom when he called her?"

"Not exactly. *She* decided the same thing. They had a big argument and she says I have to stay away."

"I don't believe it," Jess wailed. "They're both crazy! Dad's still furious about me messing up his conference this morning, and he said no way can I have another horse. He said you and your mom had weird ideas about the way to look after horses and he didn't want me having anything to do with you."

"What the heck did those two *say* to each other? I've never known my mom to get so mad," I said gloomily.

"Dad *does* wind people up," Jess admitted. "Jimmy says I'm a lot like him – just dive in and say exactly what I want without working out the best way of asking first."

"So what do we do now?" I scuffed at the ground with my boot. "How about we meet up by the cross-country course or by the river every day? That way if they find out we can pretend it was just by accident. Maybe when our fighting parents both simmer down things will get back to normal."

"Don't hold your breath," Jess warned. "Dad can be *really* stubborn."

Thinking of the determination I'd seen on my mom's face, I was dreading she might be the same.

"So what do you think of Marnie's – I mean my – idea?" I put my arm around my pony's neck. "Should we back off for a bit and just meet up in the woods or wherever?"

"Yeah that'll be good," she sighed as the phone started crackling. "How about nine tomorrow morning?"

"Yeah," I agreed. "By the cross-country jumps. No one else ever goes up there."

"OK." Her voice was fading. "I'm going back in Tag's field to keep him company."

"Good." I tried to smile. "*You're* his herd now, so I hope he soon gets used to that."

"Poor Tag," I said to Marnie after Jess had hung up. "I feel sorry for Jess, and for me, but Tag's the one who'll really suffer."

She nuzzled me affectionately and I stayed with her right up till feeding time when I grudgingly gave Mom the usual hand with our menagerie. I kept a deeply offended silence, though, not even responding when she offered to cook my favorite pancakes for dessert. Instead I had an early, silent bedtime and in the morning made sure my breakfast was a solitary one. As soon as I finished my morning chores I got Marnie ready.

"Where are you off to?" Mom spoke in an artificially bright voice.

"Cross-country," I said tersely.

"Do you want some company? Texas might like a trip out."

"He can't do jumping," I said at once. "His legs aren't up to it."

"We could go somewhere else – swimming maybe. He enjoys that."

"Marnie and I want to practice a new route we've made." I wasn't being truthful and I didn't like it, but it was *her* fault after all. "So some other time, OK?"

"Sure." Her face was a bit crumpled looking. "Sian, don't be mad at me."

"OK," I agreed politely. "See you later then."

"Do you have your phone?" She looked sad and defeated.

"Yes," I said. "The reception's not too bad from the woods, so don't worry."

She was already worrying though, and I felt pretty mean as she watched Marnie and me leave the yard. I deliberately took a different route, a longer one that didn't lead me past Danelea, but I still reached the set

81

of jumps deep in the woods before Jess did. I spent a while tidying up a couple of the jumps, helped as always by Marnie, who obligingly hauled a big branch into the different position I wanted. Just as I was starting to think Jess had forgotten the way or her dad had banned her from riding out as well as everything else, she and Tag appeared. Her small face was very pale and I noticed large sweat patches under Tag's saddlecloth and between his legs.

"What's the matter?" I moved quickly over to her. "Did you get lost? Or did Tag bolt with you? Or –"

"Oh, *Sian*!" she said – and burst into noisy, anguished tears.

Chapter Eight

While I cuddled her, leaning across from my saddle with my arms comfortingly around her, Tag pressed his handsome head against Marnie.

"L-look." Jess hiccupped between sobs. "They're hugging too."

"Tag's telling Marnie all about it." I patted her back.

"It's just – just horrible." she sniffed. "Nothing dreadful happened, I don't mean that. It's just that Tag is *so* sad and he's getting worse, not better."

"Was he calling and pacing up and down again this morning?" I fished out a clean tissue and gave it to her.

"Yeah, he started really early. I could hear him from my bedroom and Madge heard him too. She told Jimmy and we both ran down to the field, and I tried to be what you said – you know, Tag's new herd, but, but – I don't think it's *me* he wants." She gave a fresh wail and blew her nose loudly. "He's definitely calling someone else."

"It'll be a horse, not a someone." I tried to make her feel better. "He's probably always had at least one other horse with him, but he *will* get used to being alone. He just has to accept that you're herd leader, and that if you leave him he has to get on with it."

"But it doesn't have to be like this!" Jess's eyes and nose were red from crying. "My dad could put a stop to all of this by getting another horse but he won't even talk about it."

"You tried again?" I watched as Marnie nuzzled Tag into relaxing his tense muscles.

"Yes, I even held the house phone out of the window so Dad could hear Tag calling, but he doesn't know anything about horses so it didn't make any difference.

He said maybe Tag was telling me he was hungry or thirsty."

"But we know he's saying he's *lonely*," I sighed and sat back in my saddle. "Poor Tag. Did he act up when you got him out of the field?"

"Not really. He came into the yard OK, but then, I guess when he realized it was empty, he started whinnying and getting agitated. Jimmy and I put him in his stable hoping he'd calm down, but he sweated up even more and started that awful door-kicking again."

"What about the ride here? He didn't try to bolt with you or anything?"

"No." she bent forward and stroked his neck. "He tried so hard to be good, but he was nervous and jumpy. Sorry I was late. The whole thing was just such a nightmare."

Her lower lip started trembling again and I said hurriedly, "Don't worry, you're here now and Tag's starting to look more confident."

"Only because we're with you two now," she said hopelessly.

"I don't think it was Marnie he was missing this morning," I said.

"No? Then what is it? Does he just hate *me*?"

"No, he doesn't," I said strongly. "Come on, assert your leadership and ask him for some work. He'll be better when he's got something else to think about."

Tag did, indeed, improve tremendously as the morning went on and it wasn't long before Jess had him soaring confidently over the jumps in great cross-country style. He also enjoyed another cooling paddle and I cheered Jess up even more by suggesting we meet up for a real swim the following day.

"It'll wash the sweat off if he gets worked up again." She smiled bravely.

"When you get back, try a short session in the ring, riding him bareback," I suggested, "And don't forget to wear a swimsuit under your clothes tomorrow."

"OK." She looked at me. "What are you doing later today?"

"Helping move the pigs. Mom wants them to have more shade now that the weather's hot. We've got to check Danny's teeth, since they might need rasping. Then there're the ducks –"

"OK, I get the picture. Busy, busy." She grinned in her more familiar, upbeat way. "I'll probably spend the whole afternoon in Tag's field."

"I'd offer to keep you both company for an hour." I grimaced. "But I guess Jimmy's under instructions from your dad to keep me out."

"It's ridiculous." Her face darkened. "Jimmy's totally loyal, but even *he* thinks Dad has lost his marbles. But yeah, you're right, he and Madge both told me to play it cool and do everything Dad says, including staying away from you for now."

"And later?"

"When he gets back I'll be able to explain it all properly, show him stuff on the Internet about horse behavior that backs up exactly what your mom said, the works. Dad's a kind man, really. He wouldn't want Tag to be miserable; he just doesn't understand."

"Mm." I hadn't seen any sign of Christian Leyland's kind streak, but I didn't argue. "Oh well, if we can't see each other we'll just have to call or text."

"Or," a gleam came into her still red-rimmed eyes, "we could meet up without Jimmy knowing. You could sneak through that wood at the side of Tag's field and –"

"Climb up into the tree house!" I finished for her. "Yeah, that would work as long as Jimmy's not actually in the paddock."

"You text when you're on your way and I'll make sure he's not around." She'd brightened up a lot. "And I'll ask Madge for another picnic – you liked the last one."

"Great." I laughed as Marnie splashed enthusiastically through the clear water. "Tell her you're real hungry so there's plenty for both of us!"

The idea made us both laugh and it wasn't till I was back at home that I started feeling a bit guilty. I just wasn't used to having secrets from my mom. We'd always been close and shared most stuff, and I knew she hated this rift between us.

"How was your ride?" She greeted me with the same air of forced good humor.

"Good." I said. "Um –"

I was actually right on the point of telling her I'd met Jess and intended visiting her again later when she butted in, still very cheerily.

"Marvelous. You see, you and Marnie have a great time on your own. You don't need the company of that spoiled little girl next door."

"She's not a little girl," I said coldly. "She and I are the same age, and she's not spoiled either."

"Not much!" She picked up the big ginger cat who'd followed her into the yard. "The fact that her father tried to buy her an entire cross-country course just because she said she wanted one –"

"Duh! Jess didn't ask him to do that! She didn't seem to know *why* her dad came over here."

"I find that hard to believe," she sniffed. "Christian is so arrogant; he's bound to have told her. Would you believe he called again this morning, no doubt to have yet another crack at me? I just refused to listen."

"Then how do you know what he was trying to say?"

"What else would he say?" Her attitude was very irritating. "As far as he's concerned, I just don't want to know."

"Oh, suit yourself." I stalked off with my beloved pony and felt positively *glad* that I was breaking Mom's stupid new rule and sneaking off to see Jess later.

Mom followed me into the field so I could hold onto Danny, our lovely skewbald cob, while she checked his yellowing teeth.

"They're not bad, but I think I'll get the vet to take off those rough edges," she said, running her fingers gently around his mouth. "You're doing so well, aren't you

Danny, my pet? Do you remember what a bag of skin and bones he was when he first got here, Sian?"

"Yes." I deliberately turned my head away from her.

"His horrible owner said it wasn't his fault. He said, 'the horse is in a field full of grass,' but what good was that to poor Danny when he couldn't eat because his teeth were so bad? Honestly, some people just shouldn't be allowed to keep horses. That Christian Leyland, for instance –"

"Have you finished?" I still didn't look at her. "We have to move the pigs, don't we?"

She sighed and patted Danny fondly before removing his head collar so he could rejoin his friends. "OK, come on then."

It was actually difficult to do the next job without laughing. Honey and Sweet pea, our pigs, are friendly and extremely curious, always wanting to investigate anything new, so when we shepherded them out of their usual paddock they both decided to go on an exploratory walkabout. Mom, holding tight to the rope halter she was using to guide Honey, stayed with her when she took off, but ended up in a tangled heap of legs and rope when the big sow doubled back unexpectedly. I managed not to giggle as I hauled her to her feet, but when Sweet pea took the opportunity to examine the contents of a bucket she found, only to get her snout firmly stuck, I lost control and laughed all the way to the wooded field that was to be their summer home. Mom was giggling too, despite being covered in dirt and panting with exertion.

"Thanks, Sian." She gave me a brief but loving hug, and I had to remind myself I was mad at her. "Couldn't have done it without you."

The ducks are also pretty comical, and I was really starting to mellow toward Mom again, but then she made a crack about one of them behaving like a spoiled kid and it had the effect of hardening my attitude.

As soon as we were done I said, "OK, I'm off for some chill time. See you later," and set off before she could respond.

She probably expected me to head for the summer paddock and Marnie, but instead I sneaked through a gap in the hedge surrounding our house and, by cutting across the front lawn and over a low wall, was soon walking the short distance along the lane to Danelea. Remembering our arrangement, I sent Jess a text saying, *On my way, Sian*. My phone bleeped almost immediately with her reply, *OK, am in tree house, J x*. It felt a little odd, ducking out of sight behind trees as I did my best to stay hidden from view, and I didn't really like the feeling we were deceiving everyone. I said as much when I hauled myself up onto the central platform of oak branches.

Jess sniffed disparagingly and handed me a drink. "It's their own fault! Well, not Jimmy or Madge, they're just doing what their boss tells them, but my dad and your mom *deserve* to be deceived!"

"That's true," I agreed, wondering whether to mention the "Jess is a spoiled brat" remark. "I'm hardly talking to my mom, I'm so mad about this stupid ban."

"Hah! What do they know? We got around it anyway." She leaned back against the tree trunk. "I'm glad you're here. I like keeping Tag company, but – well he doesn't *say* a lot."

"Marnie does," I said a bit smugly before adding. "Well, no I guess she doesn't. I just like to think she does."

"I've been up here for twenty minutes or so." Jess parted the leaves and looked down into the paddock. "I told Tag where I was going and told him not to worry and so far he hasn't."

"That's good." I put my drink down and shifted so I could see him too. "Yeah *really* good. He's just grazing quietly and –"

As we watched, Tag's head came up sharply and he swung around twice, his eyes searching every corner of the field. With a loud whicker he set off toward the perimeter fence, swerving nervously as he went.

"Oh, no," Jess groaned. "He'll start patrolling up and down and calling next."

The bay horse did exactly that, in a jerky half walking, half jogging gait that looked very uncomfortable.

"Call him, Jess," I suggested. "Just try letting him know you're around."

She called and whistled several times, but the agitated pony didn't seem to hear her. It wasn't until she climbed down from the oak tree and went across to him that he stopped. Even then he couldn't seem to settle, and it brought a lump to my throat to see the distress in the horse's body language graphically echoed by the expression on Jess's unhappy face. I watched them for a long time, wishing desperately that I could help but not daring to join her in case Madge or Jimmy saw me and told Christian. I knew discovery would cause more trouble, not just for me but for Jess and Tag, but it still felt horrible just sitting there watching her and her beautiful pony suffer. Eventually Tag gave up and allowed Jess to lead him back to the shade of the oak tree, but they both looked dispirited and low.

"Jess," I called as soon as she was near enough. "Well done. You soothed him, and he'll be all right now."

"Just till the next time." She didn't look up at me as she spoke and her voice was flat and dreary. "You might as well go, Sian, sorry."

"No, I don't want to. Come on, climb back up and we'll chat to Tag from up here. He might settle better if he can hear us."

She did as I said, but even though my strange idea worked reasonably well, with Tag grazing in the shade under the tree while we talked to him from the tree house above, it wasn't, as Jess pointed out, a long-term solution.

"I can hardly spend every minute of every day with him, can I?" She gave me the rest of her picnic. "And I think Madge would notice if I move my bed and sleep up here as well."

"Mm." I couldn't think of anything to suggest. "I

probably spend more time than most with my pony, but when I'm not there she's all right because she's not on her own."

"You really think that's it? I'm worrying Tag's missing his old owner – that he just hasn't taken to me."

"I'm positive that isn't it," I said firmly. "But if you're so worried, why not give the previous owner a call?"

"You think?" She frowned and said slowly, "I guess I could. Then, when Dad gets home I'll have a fully researched case for him – with proof of Tag's needs."

"Well, it might be better to approach him a little more gently." I could imagine Christian's reaction if his daughter summoned him as if to a court of law.

"No!" Jess's eyes glittered. "I'm going to find out everything I can and then hit him with the evidence!"

I sighed deeply and spent the next half hour trying to persuade her that this was not a good idea, but deep down I knew I wouldn't win. Jess was on a mission and it could only mean one thing – and that was more, *much* more, trouble!

Chapter Nine

All evening I dreaded that Christian, having listened
to his daughter's latest commands, would call and give
Mom's ear another blasting. So when he actually did,
and she again refused to talk to him, I was relieved. She
made several attempts to start a conversation with me,
but when all I did was grunt in response, she gave up.
I flew through the next morning's chores, then grabbed
my swimming stuff and rushed off to get Marnie ready.
I didn't want Mom to know I was taking my pony

swimming in case she wanted to come along as well. Again I felt a pang of guilt about the deception, but told myself to get over it. Jess and I met in the woods leading to the galloping trail and, like the previous day, both she and Tag looked jittery.

"He's definitely getting worse. It's like he's constantly looking for someone." Her little face was very sad.

"Did you call his old owner?" I asked.

"He wasn't in, so I left a message asking him to call me."

"OK," I said. "There's a clearing ahead. We'll do a few dressage steps to make Tag concentrate and forget his worries. He needs to remember you're his leader, so think positive!"

Jess worked hard and got the bay pony going beautifully, which also had the effect of making them both relax.

"That's better." I grinned at her. "You're not wound up in a tight little ball now."

"It feels good. Can we give Tag some fun as well? I want him to enjoy himself when he's with me."

"Come on, then." I put a nicely warmed-up Marnie into a canter as we took the winding path lading out of the woods.

"Hah!" Jess shouted from behind us. "Tag's changing his legs so often it feels like we're dancing!"

"And in a minute we'll be flying." I glanced over my shoulder to see the two of them in perfect harmony. "Isn't it great!"

The gallop was perfect, and I could feel the power surging from my terrific pony as we raced across the turf. Tag, too, was skimming along, and only the rhythmic pounding of hooves told us our horses' feet were actually making contact with the ground. It was definitely more like flying. After admiring the view of the valley, we started the long slope downward again. Jess jumped Tag over anything and everything. Now that he'd settled down he was demonstrating just what a fabulous horse he was, and I was glad to see how totally happy they both looked. It felt good to enter the cool shade approaching the river, and as we came out into the sunlight again, the magical, shimmering stretch of water had never looked more inviting.

"OK." Jess's eyes were shining. "Tell me how to do this."

"Saddles off, obviously, plus your own boots and breeches."

"Should I keep my T-shirt on?" She copied the way I stowed my saddle against a tree.

"It'll get wet if you do." I was just wearing my swimsuit. "This is proper swimming, remember."

"OK." Holding onto Tag's reins, she looked around, perplexed. "How do we mount? Do I stand on something?"

"You vault onto Tag's back." I demonstrated on my own pony. "Like in Pony Club games."

"I've never tried it." She tried now, but slithered back down Tag's side again.

"Hold the reins in your left hand on his withers, with your right on the other side of his neck," I instructed. "Now push off with both feet, springing upwards and swinging your right leg over."

It took her three more attempts, but she managed, and the beam on her face said it all. "Wow, having no saddle feels amazing."

"You didn't practice in the ring like I told you?"

She shook her head. "Sorry, I was too busy trying to keep Tag happy. We're both fine with it though."

"Good." I really hoped so. "Do you want to ride around for a bit before we go into the river?"

"Nah. Let's do it!"

Tag followed Marnie readily, with Jess wisely giving him plenty of time to move into the deeper channel.

"Stay near us," I advised. "It's a gentle current along here, but not so much if you go further out."

"OK." Her eyes were wide as she watched Marnie plunge confidently forward. "Oh, you're swimming, you're actually – Oh wow, Sian, so are we!"

Tag had taken off so smoothly that Jess had barely noticed his hooves leave the riverbed.

"It's cold," she laughed. "And sort of silky against my legs. Oh, and Tag feels like an otter or a seal, all smooth and slippery."

"He's loving it." I'd turned to watch them.

"Yes." She closed her eyes in sheer bliss. "And so am I!"

Marnie, who was also having a wonderful time, powered strongly to a point where the channel deepened and I turned her in a wide arc, pushing her back toward the quieter stretch we'd already swum through. Jess, copying our every move, did the same, but as Tag swung around, she slipped sideways.

"Grab a handful of mane and pull yourself back on," I called. "Just –"

But Jess, panicking a little, had lost her grip completely and, pushed back by the surge of water as Tag changed direction, she dropped the reins and slithered awkwardly into the deep channel of the river. Tag, blithely following Marnie, seemed unaware at first and just kept on swimming.

"Help!" Jess spluttered as she ducked under the surface and took in a great gulp of water. "Tag! Come to me!"

Despite being a good swimmer she sounded suddenly scared, but before I could turn my pony and swim back to her Tag took over. Ears flickering, he took another turn, powering his legs through the river till he was facing Jess again.

"Tag," she cried again and he answered – a brave, whickering call that said clearly, "I'm on my way!"

Within moments he had reached her, swimming beside her till she managed to clamber, somewhat clumsily, onto his sleek, wet back.

"Wow, Jess." I got Marnie to take us back to the shallows. "Wasn't he *fantastic*!"

"He saved me." As Tag took a few steps to join us she leaned forward and hugged him dramatically. "Tag came back and saved me."

"Uh, well," I demurred. "You weren't exactly going to drown, were you?"

"I know that," she said, still cuddling her pony. "But Tag didn't. All he knew was that I needed help, and he came straight back to me."

"That's pretty special," I agreed. "So you can stop all that negative stuff about him not taking to you. Tag already loves you. He's just shown how much."

There were tears in her eyes. "That makes me so happy I could – I could –"

"Swim some more?" I suggested, grinning.

"Sure," she said at once. "Only this time I'll stay on board!"

We had a great time, and by the time we returned to dry land Jess and Tag were swimming together as though they'd been born to it. We let both ponies shake the majority of water off them, then used the towels we'd brought to dry all four of us as best we could.

"The sun will do the rest," I said. "While we have a bite to eat."

"Sorry, I didn't know I was supposed to bring anything."

"No, it's my turn to provide the picnic, though it's not up to Madge's standards." I pulled four apples, a packet of cookies and a drink from my backpack and told Tag, "Grass and an apple for you and your friend, and cookies and an apple for me and *my* friend."

It was just perfect, lying back on the sweet smelling grass with the warm sun shining from a high, azure sky, the gentle murmur of the river mingling with bird song and the soft rustling of leaves in a summer breeze. I was so full of joy and peace as Marnie and I made our way back home that I decided to stop being mad at Mom and tell her everything.

"Once she hears how devoted Jess is to Tag and how hard she's trying to make him happy, she'll realize how stupid this ban is," I told my pony. "Because Mom is a kind and reasonable person."

But as far as Christian Leyland was concerned, Mom was not prepared to be kind *or* reasonable.

"No, Sian," she said firmly. "When I said you were to keep out of this I meant it. Mr. Leyland made it very clear he didn't want any interference from us."

"But Jess is really struggling –" I began.

"It's none of our business." She held out her hand. "I told you that and you deliberately ignored me. If I can't trust you not to contact Jess I'm confiscating your phone."

"What?" I couldn't believe it.

"Give it to me please." She put it in a drawer, and *locked* it.

I gaped at her open-mouthed. "That is so UNFAIR. I'm bound to meet Jess anyway. She knows where I ride now."

"If that's your intention then you're grounded." The two bright circles of anger flared up on her cheeks again. "You'll have to exercise Marnie in our ring for the next three days."

"No way!" I was shocked. She never grounds me. "Why are you being like this?"

"Jess's father said he didn't want his daughter influenced by what he considers our sentimental approach to animals. He could not have made it plainer, Sian, and now I'm spelling it out for you. You are to stay away from Danelea, from Jess and from her horse. Do you understand?"

"I understand two so-called adults are ruining Jess's and my lives because they don't like each other," I shouted. "*We're* the kids, so how come it's you and Christian who are the ones acting childish?"

"That's enough," she said and turned away.

"No it's not," I yelled at her back. "You've always worked hard to teach people the right way to treat their animals. Why is Christian so different?"

"For one thing," she said, throwing the words over her shoulder, "he's not being cruel. You told me Tag is being well cared for, and for another – well maybe he's right, Sian, maybe I have turned into a self-righteous, interfering madwoman."

"Madwoman?" I lowered my voice. "Is that what he called you? Oh, he didn't mean it. He was still fuming about the conference. Jess says he's –"

But she was gone. I walked slowly out of the house and back, of course, to Marnie. I spent most of the next two days with her, in fact, moping around her field in between schooling sessions and feeding times. There was a chilly restraint between Mom and me, but now instead of me doing the sulking it seemed to be mostly her. My phone stayed locked away, and being grounded meant I couldn't leave Greylodge's grounds, so there was no way of getting in touch with Jess. All I could do was hope she was coping and that she'd worked out why I'd suddenly dropped out of her life. I thought my Mom's attitude would soften, but nothing seemed to be

changing until, on the third day, I was walking back from
Marnie when the big, powerful car belonging to Christian
pulled up outside our front door. I ducked quickly inside
the back one, running through the kitchen and into the
hall so I could find out what was going on. I stood back
a little, keeping out of sight, and saw Mom come out of
her studio to answer the doorbell. Being behind her, I
obviously couldn't see her face but I could imagine the
expression on it when she saw Christian.

"Mr. Leyland." Her hand automatically flew to her
hair which, thankfully, didn't have a sock in it.

"Christian," he said, also automatically. "I decided to
call on you in person because you just won't talk to me
on the phone anymore. Kim – I – have you seen –"

"You'd better come in," She led him to the studio so,
still in spy mode, I crept quietly along the hall.

From a vantage point by the door I could see Christian
and I was shocked at how haggard he looked.

"First of all, I want to say what I've been trying to
tell you on the phone." He ran a hand nervously through
his hair. "I'm – I'm really sorry I said all those horrible
things the other day. I was in a rage about the way Jess
interrupted my work and I took it out on you. She's

always been headstrong, but she's never done anything like that before and I was stupid enough to blame you. I'm sorry."

"Oh." Mom sounded quite taken aback. "Thank you. I didn't realize that was what you called to say, so *I'm* sorry I wouldn't listen. I don't know Jess, of course, but from what Sian has told me, I think your daughter is genuinely worried about her horse."

"Yes she is. When I got back this morning she started right in about Tag. She's spoken to Bob Granger who sold him to us, and he thinks Tag's unhappiness can only be solved by being reunited with the horse he always lived with. The horse is called Freddie, and – uh – Bob did offer him to me when I paid for Tag but I said no. I thought Jess only needed one horse, but Bob assured her it's Freddie that Tag is missing."

"I'm not sure about that." Mom's voice was soft now. "Tag would probably get used to a new companion, but it does sound as though company is what he needs."

"I don't know anything about horses, and the trouble is," Christian's shoulders slumped, "I was still mad at Jess and said I definitely wouldn't do it. Jess is like me in many ways, too strong willed and opinionated –"

"So what happened? Why are you here?"

"She's gone," he said simply. "Madge came to find me because Jess told her if I wouldn't sort Tag's problem out *she* would. When I saw she'd taken the horse, I assumed she'd come here."

"No, I'm afraid not," Mom said, chewing her lip, I could tell. "I – I was angry too and I banned Sian from seeing her. I even took Sian's phone away."

"There where could Jess be?" There was real panic in Christian's eyes.

"She's probably just gone for a ride to cool down." Mom tried to soothe him. "She'll be back soon, I'm sure."

I, on the other hand, wasn't. I had the strong feeling that if Jess thought her father wouldn't change his mind about helping her beloved horse she really *would* do something about it. Silently I moved back down the hall and out of the house. The only place she might have left a clue was at Danelea and there was no time to waste. I raced along the lane, and took the secret route through the woods to the oak tree at the back of Tag's paddock. Jess had made some additions to the tree house: a box containing two plastic cups, a pen and notepad, another chair, and her folder on horse care. I opened it hurriedly and flicked through the pages. At the back was an address and phone number, *Bob Granger, Dunford Farm, Brackenbury*. I recognized the name at once, and knew Brackenbury was a village on the other side of our valley. I could see Jess knew that too. She'd sketched a rough map of the route.

"It's the place they bought Tag from," I told myself. "Jess is going there to bring Tag's old friend Freddie back."

I'm not like Jess; I don't do impulsive things and I always think things through, but I was so fired up I hardly paused to think at all. Jess had never ridden so far on her own before, so she needed my support and that was all that mattered. I was back down the tree in a flash, running full out through the woods, back down the lane and into Greylodge's yard. Christian's car was still outside the front door, but even if he and Mom had come outside and seen me, I'd still have raced to get Marnie ready, still have moved her swiftly out of the yard and into the woods leading to the galloping trail. Marnie had no idea why I was in such a hurry, and she was positively delighted. She'd had two dull days, so the prospect of a fast paced outing suited her mood exactly. It had to be fast – we needed to catch up with Jess and Tag and we had a long, long way to go!

Chapter Ten

I knew the route pretty well. I'd joined in a Pony Club trek earlier in the year and we'd passed Brackenbury on the ride. It was almost a straight line once you were out of the valley, so I was confident Jess, who'd no doubt researched it, would find her way, all right. The only tricky part was crossing the river that cut through the terrain on the other side of the hill. There was, our Club leader told us, only one really safe place to cross; a broad, shallow ford. To reach it we'd had to divert from the trail we'd followed most of the way and circle a scrubby piece of land that looked as though it led nowhere. It was easy to take the wrong route there, so I wanted to catch up with Jess before she reached it.

"If we don't get to her she might try swimming across," I spoke worriedly to Marnie. "And although she and Tag did well the other day, this isn't the same thing. There's a strong current in that part of the river, and – well, we have to try and reach them before they get that far."

My lovely pony was certainly eager to help. She'd taken the galloping trail in her usual exuberant style, but instead of traveling the downward slope back into our valley I'd kept her on the hill above it, moving forward at a steady canter. The high country surrounding Greylodge and Danelea is the reason for our poor cell phone reception, blocking or even interrupting the signal. It didn't concern me much today of course, because my phone was still locked away in the house. Just thinking about the way Mom had taken it from me made me grit my teeth. This frantic chase wouldn't be necessary if I could call Jess and tell her to wait for me. There was nothing to do now except to keep going, maintaining the pace so that Marnie's hooves ate up the ground beneath us. It wasn't too long before we were at the far side of the hill where it began its gradual descent into another, bigger valley. Ahead the trail shelved quite steeply, and the ground was uneven and stony, so I slowed her to walk, giving her a long rein so she could carefully pick her own way to the grassy vale below.

"Brackenbury is about four miles down the other side of the river," I told Marnie. "The ford where we cross is probably only two or three miles from here."

She flicked her ears, seeming to understand the need for our urgency, and began cantering along the springy green trail, with me peering ahead, hoping and praying I'd soon catch sight of Jess and Tag. To make things worse the weather was changing. The sun was now hidden behind a thick blanket of cloud and the light summer breeze was building to a heavy gust.

"Oh, don't rain!" I begged. "I'm only wearing a T-shirt, and I bet Jess hasn't got wet weather stuff on."

Slowing down as we passed through the woods, I tried looking down at the ground to see if there was any sign that Jess and Tag had passed this way. There were hoof prints in a damp patch of earth and some droppings, but I didn't know if they were fresh, as in minutes old, or maybe from another horse altogether, so neither sign was much help. The valley was very quiet; even the cheerful chink of bird song had ceased as the bad weather closed in. The wind was beginning to shake the treetops as it tore at their branches above us. The woods were becoming a dark world of rattling twigs and moaning sighs of the wind, so I urged Marnie onwards, even more anxious to find Jess and Tag before they reached the river. At last we were through and out into open country again, but even here the clouds, heavy and black now, dimmed the light and I could no longer search in the distance for the longed-for sight of my friend and her beautiful bay horse. Spots of rain began falling as my loyal pony surged forward into a canter. Then the light gray dapple of her coat was quickly darkened as the skies opened, sending ice-cold torrents that soaked her skin. I was drenched too. My T-shirt and breeches already clung to me uncomfortably, but there was no time to stop and find shelter. At last the trail curved away toward the scrubby piece of land I remembered, and straight ahead was the river. I could hear it clearly, its musical tinkle now a muted roar as, swept by the storm, it surged between steep banks on either side. Still worrying that Jess might think she and Tag had to cross this deep stretch in order to reach Brackenbury, I tried to brush the worst of the rain from my eyes.

"We'd better check the river out first, Marnie," I yelled above the raging sounds of storm and river. "We have to make sure they haven't taken the wrong route."

We moved toward the fast running river as I desperately scanned both sides for any sign of Jess and Tag. Even without the storm, this stretch of river was scary enough. Now, however, with its swift current and deep, steel-gray water pitted and scarred by lashing rain while the wind whipped the surface into white foam, the thought of swimming across it was truly terrifying.

"Jess wouldn't have risked Tag in there, surely?" I bent my soaked, wind battered head low against Marnie's neck. "She loves him too much, I know she does."

Marnie whickered, turning her fine head, and I patted her soaking wet shoulder. "You're right, we'll turn back and check out the ford. They're probably already through it and —"

My pony's sensitive ears had heard something even above the fearsome clatter of the storm. For a moment she stood quite still. Then, instead of turning back as

I'd intended, she moved toward a small clump of trees huddling a short distance from the river's edge.

"Marnie?" I recognized her purposeful gait. There was something she wanted me to see so I let her take me. The group of trees provided welcome shelter, a small oasis from the brunt of the storm, and I was able to wipe the rain from my eyes.

"There's nothing." I peered through the gloom. "Nothing."

Marnie shook her head, sending clouds of raindrops cascading from her mane, and whickered, the soft, long note she used to comfort. To my amazement a short way ahead I heard an answering, more panicky call that I recognized immediately as Tag. Marnie pushed her way through a tangle of undergrowth and there, his reins caught in thorny brambles, was Tag, his eyes shining in the gloomy half-light.

"Tag!" It only took a moment to reach him, but several more to disentangle the reins from the spiky, clinging branches.

He was wet, of course, though not as soaked as Marnie and I were.

"You must have been caught up in here for a while."

I stroked his neck gently. "And you definitely haven't been in the river, thank goodness."

My fear that Jess had taken the wrong route seemed to be correct, but at least she and her horse weren't battling their way through the strong current I could hear roaring past us.

"Where is she?" I crooned soothingly to the bay pony. "I really wish you could talk, Tag."

It seemed mean to ask both horses to leave the shelter of trees, but we had to find Jess. We were still dangerously close to the river, and I wanted to find her quickly, to make sure she was safe. Tag let me lead him, pushing his nose against Marnie as we plodded our way along the bank. Soon we could go no further. The way ahead was impassable as the river rounded a rocky outcrop and disappeared from view.

"We'll go back to the trail and find the ford," I told the two horses. "Come on, Marnie, turn around and –"

Again she stood stock still, her intelligent ears pricked forward. I could barely see a thing through the heavy curtain of rain, but as I inched forward I realized what she had spotted – a small, huddled figure almost hidden behind a rock.

"Jess!" I flung myself out of the saddle and knelt beside her.

She was soaked through and her out-flung hand was icy cold when I touched it.

"Oh, Jess!" Now tears mingled with the rain pouring down my face. "Wake up, please wake up."

Tag, still close beside Marnie, bent to look at the small, still figure, his warm breath lifting her hair as he nuzzled gently into her neck. She stirred then, a mere fluttering of her eyelids and a slight movement as she turned her face toward him. He moved his soft lips across her cheek and this time her eyes opened fully.

"T-Tag." Her voice was a whisper, but as the bay pony nuzzled against her skin she said his name again, more strongly.

"Yes, it's Tag." I tried to gulp away my tears as she managed to sit up and reach for her pony. "He's worried that you're hurt."

"I'm not sure I am." Stiffly she clambered to her feet and leaned against Tag, wrapping her arms around his neck.

I let them hug for a few moments, then guided them slowly back to the comparative shelter of trees. Jess and I were both shivering, but in the dim light under the canopy of leaves I could see she was very pale, her lips almost blue. I knew she needed help and that we had to move to find it. Somehow we managed to get her into Tag's saddle, with me using all my strength to lift and push as she struggled.

"I know we're probably nearer Brackenbury than home." Because Jess had no strength I was still leading Tag. "But I think we should turn back – you need to be home."

"No." She could hardly speak, but she meant it. "Dunford Farm, Bob Granger, that's where we have to go."

"But you're not well," I protested. "You can't possibly take this other horse home with you."

"Not going to," she gasped. "Dad won't get another one, so I'm taking Tag back to his friend Freddie. I want him to be happy."

As I stared open-mouthed she closed her eyes, swaying as she tried to keep a grip on Tag's mane.

"Jess," I said urgently. "You need help. Do you have your phone?"

She nodded slowly and fumbled for it. "Call Bob." she handed it to me. "Tell him we're coming."

I peered at the cold, wet phone, praying it was still working. To my relief there was a signal, but when I called the keyed in number, Bob Granger's answering machine responded and my spirits plummeted. Croaking a little, I stuttered out the story, that Jess and I were on our way to return the lonely Tag so he could be with Freddie, and then slumped in my saddle, feeling more helpless than I ever had in my life. Even under the tree cover we were still getting soaked, the storm raging relentlessly around us.

"Let's go." I made a decision. "The ford's not far."

Jess's eyes were still shut and her skin looked pale and waxy.

I wanted to tie her onto the saddle but had nothing to tie her with, so all I could do was say, "Hold tight, Jess," as I moved Marnie forward.

Going back out into the maelstrom of beating rain and howling wind was a nightmare and I was proud of the way both horses tackled it. We plodded, heads down against the storm, back to the trail, this time heading toward the ford. It was a ten minute trudge through the circle of scrubland that I realized must skirt the impassable rocky outcrop on the river bank. The storm was at its height, lashing and screaming at us, and when we reached the ford I knew we were beaten. What had been a broad, but tranquil, stretch of shallow river was now a raging torrent and though still not deep, the sheer force of water as it roared past us made crossing absolutely impossible. Stricken, I punched in my home number on Jess's phone, but the number was busy, even after several tries. Glancing anxiously at Jess's ashen face I tried the Dunford Farm number again – only for the machine to answer once more. Trapped on one side by the river, behind us the long, uphill trek home, I just didn't know what to do. Marnie decided for me. Turning her back resolutely on the raging water, she set off.

"Where – what?" Jess sounded half asleep.

"It's OK." I forced myself to sound positive. "We can't cross here so it's plan B. Just stay awake and in the saddle. If you fall off –"

"I won't," she managed to say, and I tightened my grip on Tag's reins.

This time the wind and rain were behind us, just as fierce, cold and wet, but at least now I could see a little. The journey, ridden on the way here at a hot racing pace, now seemed to take forever. Marnie was magnificent, making steady, determined progress, and as we crested the hill and were heading toward our own valley I felt real hope. I'd been dreading meeting the full force of the storm high on that exposed summit but it was, at last, abating. Tag, carefully carrying the semi-conscious Jess, was wonderful too, keeping steady as a rock as he followed us trustingly through it all. Both ponies raised their heads as the wind dropped and the icy needles of rain turned to drizzle. The most direct route home was down our galloping trail, and we'd never taken that stretch of turf so slowly. Jess, swaying a little on the incline, opened her eyes a few times but was too weak to ask where we were. She was only just holding on and as we reached the last, longed-for stage of our journey I realized my own strength was fast running out too. When Marnie called her greeting whinny and an anxious human voice answered, I closed my eyes and let myself slide, down, down into the warm, loving arms of my mom.

◆ ◆ ◆ ◆

The next half hour was a blur of lovely hot bath water, thick towels and cozy comforter. Once I was in bed Mom brought me soup, crusty bread and a drink and left me with strict instructions to do nothing but eat, drink and rest.

"But Marnie –" I tried to struggle out. "I have to –"

"She's already rugged up in *her* nice bed with a warm mash to eat," Mom said. "So, STAY WHERE YOU ARE! I'm going to check on her and Tag. I'll be back in a minute."

The food, warmth and comfort were just what I needed, so when she came back I was feeling much, much better.

"Both horses are fine." She smiled at me.

"Tag is here?" I asked. "Won't that make Christian angry?"

"Christian asked me to keep Tag. He's driven Jess to the hospital. She's suffering from hypothermia and has a bump on the head."

"She was unconscious when we found her." I gave Mom a run down of the horrendous journey. "Poor Jess will be devastated that she didn't reach Dunford Farm. She was taking Tag there, you see, taking him back to be with his friend."

"Freddie." Mom nodded. "I know. Bob Granger called Christian when he heard your message. We just didn't know what to do. The storm was raging and you were both somewhere out there where we couldn't follow. Bob said he'd check his side of the river, but he didn't think you'd be able to use the ford. Christian wanted to search over here, of course, and was nearly out of his mind with worry. I was just saddling up Texas so I could try to find you when we heard Marnie call."

"She was brilliant," I said proudly. "Just brilliant."

"And so were you," Mom's eyes suddenly filled with tears. "I'm so sorry I got it all wrong, Sian. I blamed Christian for being arrogant, but I was just as bad."

"You were both pretty bad," I agreed. "But we all make mistakes."

She laughed then and tickled me till I begged for mercy.

Jess had to stay in the hospital for two days, even though she said after the first night she felt fine.

"They've done tons of tests," she told me when I visited her. "Because I banged my head on a rock, I guess."

"It's probably to make sure you still have a brain." I grinned. "Not that you had much of one to start with!"

"Thanks, pal," she said. "And *real* thanks for, you know, rescuing me."

"That was mostly Marnie. And Tag. He really looked after you."

"How – how is he?"

"OK." I nodded. "He's still at Greylodge, sharing a field with his girlfriend and our other horses."

"I bet he loves that." Her face lit up. "Or does he still call for Freddie?"

"Not so often, but yes, he still misses him." I changed the subject quickly. "Can I come visit you when you get home tomorrow? My Mom has lifted the ban."

"So has my dad." She smiled. "He even said he was sorry for being such a dork."

"So did my mom!" I looked at her and we both burst out laughing.

To my surprise when Christian went to get her from hospital the next day he asked me if I'd go with him.

"I think Jess would like it if you're with me." He looked different, wearing old jeans instead of a formal business suit, and much nicer now that he was smiling.

"Sure," I said at once. "If Mom doesn't need me to help around here."

"No, I'm fine." She was smiling too. "I'll see you all later."

I looked over at the horses as we drove away and saw poor Tag standing at the gate, calling hopefully toward the yard. He was obviously still missing Freddie and I opened my mouth to ask what Christian planned to do about him, then decided it still wasn't any of my business so closed it again. Jess was waiting, dressed and raring to go when we reached the ward, and was impatient when her dad spent time talking to the staff.

"I was just saying thank you," he defended himself when at last we were leaving. "For looking after you so well. You're not exactly the easiest person in the world, are you?"

"I behaved perfectly." She glared at him. "Stuck in here, what else *could* I do?"

"And whose fault was it that you ended up in the hospital?"

"Hey, you two," I butted in. "I thought you were pleased to be going home together, yet you're already starting another fight!"

"Sorry, Sian." Christian ruffled his daughter's hair. "It's become a bit of a habit. We'll have to agree to always agree, won't we Jess?"

"Yeah right," she pretended to grumble. "Like *that's* going to happen!"

They kept up the banter all the way home, and though

I could see they didn't mean the barbs I just wished they'd tell each other how they really felt.

"OK." Christian swung the car into Danelea's drive. "What first? Something to eat? Watch TV? Or –"

"Duh! Straight to the yard or the field, wherever Tag is." Jess caught her breath. "Unless he's back at Dunford Farm?"

"He was at Greylodge when we left," I told her, "but I didn't see him in the field when we passed just now."

"Really?" Christian wasn't a very good actor. "Then where could he be?"

I was as eager as Jess to jump out of the car and run through the yard to the field. To my surprise there was my mom, standing by the gate.

"Tag!" Jess didn't notice anything except her horse. "Tag, come –" she broke off and stared.

Across the grass the beautiful bay pony had turned at the sound of her voice and he came cantering, every sinew alive with joy, straight toward her. Behind him, not moving with quite such style and grace, followed a piebald cob, a little plain and clumsy, but quite obviously delighted to be with his friend.

"Freddie!" Jess squealed. "I saw him when we bought Tag. It's Freddie! Oh, *Dad*!"

"I was very touched by the fact you'd rather give up your beloved horse than let him be unhappy," Christian said quietly. "I'm proud of you, Jess."

"You're just the best!" She was crying and hugging him and *both* ponies all at the same time.

Mom and I stood back, smiling at the four of them.

"You knew?" I looked at her and she nodded.

"Christian asked me to bring Tag here and wait for Freddie's trailer to arrive. They were both so pleased to see each other that I was worried they might not even greet Jess, but –"

"But Tag loves *me* too." Jess's face was aglow with happiness.

"I can see that." Christian was patting both horses. "And I'm glad you all made me see that it's not just us humans who need company."

"That's right." Mom smiled quite sweetly at him. "And *I'm* glad you did something about it once you believed that horses really do get lonely too!"